Secrets of Sugarcreek
✚
THE QUIET

Soldier

Secrets of Sugarcreek

✝

THE QUIET

Soldier

SERENA B. MILLER

Edited by
HANNAH MILLER

LJ EMORY
PUBLISHING

Author photos by Angie Griffith and KMK Photography

KMKphotography.com - Used by permission.

Cover & Interior design by Jacob Miller

Published by L. J. Emory Publishing

First L. J. Emory Publishing trade paperback edition Nov 2025

ISBN 978-1-940283-88-3 (eBook Version)

ISBN 978-1-940283-87-6 (Print Version)

"Yea, though I walk through
the valley of the shadow of death,
I will fear no evil:
for thou art with me;
thy rod and thy staff they comfort me."

~PSALM 23:4 (KJV)

"We were so tired of
death and destruction;
we wanted to do something beautiful."

~COL. CHARLES REED,
CDR., 2ND CAV GROUP,
U.S. ARMY, 1945

*To the faithful team at
the Gospel Book Store in Berlin, Ohio—
past and present—
whose encouragement has lifted countless
authors and whose service has blessed
the Holmes County, Amish,
and Christian communities for years.*

PROLOGUE

E ven in small Ohio villages—where everyone's business is everyone's business—secrets still manage to stay hidden. They hide behind jars of homemade applesauce in immaculate pantries, bury themselves in crumbling cardboard boxes hidden in forgotten attics, and cower beneath frayed Amish quilts hoping no one will ever discover them.

I am Amy Stanton, twenty-nine, a ghostwriter, and a professional teller of other people's secrets. In other words, I make my living helping people write their autobiographies.

Until ten months ago, I was a dedicated New Yorker with a rent-controlled apartment in Manhattan that I defended like territory in a war zone.

Then my favorite ex-stepfather, Rick Downey, passed away and left his estate to me. This consists of a two-hundred-acre farm near Sugarcreek, Ohio, a flock of chickens led by a demonic rooster named Zedekiah, and a strange new existence where my closest friends wear suspenders and prayer *kapps*.

I also inherited an antique shop crammed with treasure. Rick had been an appraiser at Sotheby's. He knew the value of old things, and I did not. The idea of ever opening that store for business scared me to death. I couldn't tell the difference between true depression glassware and a cheap knockoff. Which is why, ten months later, the store remains closed while I figure out what to do with it. The nagging fear of accidentally selling a fifty-thousand-dollar ashtray for fifty cents haunts me.

I had intended to inventory Rick's estate, list the property, and escape back to civilization as soon as possible. Instead, I found myself inexplicably drawn to this rural corner of Ohio, with its patchwork of tidy farms, the clip-clop of horse-drawn buggies, and a community bound by traditions that I still struggle to understand.

Then I met Lucas Hershberger, the stoic Amish farmer who managed Rick's land with unassuming competence. He was stubborn, principled, occasionally maddening—and somehow the person I most wanted to talk to at the end of each day.

Lucas helped introduce me to this community's rhythm of seasons and faith, where helping neighbors isn't just kindness but survival. Living here initially felt like an idyllic existence, but as I've got to know the area better, I've learned that even the most peaceful people carry unspoken shadows from their past.

My farm manager is widowed and Amish. I'm single and not. At first, I was simply grateful to have inherited the help of such a competent employee. Then, before I even realized what was happening, I fell in love with him.

The Amish don't marry outside their faith. I didn't know how serious they were about this until he casually mentioned that it was time for him to begin his search for an Amish wife.

I didn't argue. Like a frightened rabbit, I scurried back to New York City where I wouldn't have to watch him break my heart.

Back in the city, I threw myself into work, convincing myself I belonged in the fast-paced, anonymous embrace of Manhattan—where nobody's transportation required hay.

But in the dark hours before dawn, when even the city seemed to hold its breath, I missed the small moments of life in the hills of rural Ohio: the sound of Zedekiah crowing in the morning, the sight of laundry drying on lines, watching Lucas plow fields and train horses with competency and grace.

In the meantime, my mother, Desiree Stanton, a world-famous actress, occasionally blew through my life like a category 4 hurricane.

However, thanks to the letter that Rick left me, I discovered some unsettling truths about her past that made me wonder if I had ever known her at all.

I thought I had put Sugarcreek—and my feelings for Lucas—far behind me.

It took only one phone call for me to discover I was wrong.

CHAPTER 1

I was with my editor, Carolyn Walsh, at the Palm Court at the Plaza Hotel when my phone buzzed. I ignored it. She and I were having a pleasant lunch while talking about possibilities for our next writing project, and I didn't want to be interrupted.

I selected a tiny, crustless, cucumber sandwich from the finger foods displayed on the tray beside us and nibbled it while refilling my delicate teacup with the pot of hot tea sitting in front of me. I'd chosen the Plaza's Signature Blend, and it was delicious. Carolyn had the Chai Imperial, and the spicy aroma wafting from it had me wishing I had chosen that one instead. Maybe next time.

My cell phone buzzed again.

I'd been getting too many scam calls recently, so I ignored it. If it were important, whoever it was would leave a message.

"I'm sorry, Amy. I have to leave you for a few minutes," Carolyn said apologetically. "This tea is going straight through me."

"Of course," I said. "Please take your time."

Going to the restroom from the Palm Court was a bit of a trek. There was a long corridor, a stairwell leading down to the basement, and then more walking. I felt sorry for anyone who needed to get there quickly.

I was pouring another cup of tea when the phone buzzed a third time. That worried me enough to dig my cell phone out of my purse and glance at the number. The area code was 330, which meant it was someone calling from Sugarcreek. My pulse quickened as I answered it.

It was Erma.

"I don't know if I should make this call," she said. "It's probably a mistake, but Lucas…"

She choked up, and my heart tightened with fear.

"What about Lucas?"

"He's been hurt."

"What do you mean? What happened?"

"Well." Erma took a deep breath and started in. "Ida Schrock came to town with her daughter, Charity. Ida has dementia, and Charity can't hardly do a thing with her anymore, poor thing. She's afraid to leave her mother at home alone, but taking her with her to do errands is getting iffy."

"Tell me about Lucas, Erma."

"That's what I'm trying to do!" Erma said. "Ida refused to get out of the buggy. She's been getting combative recently. Charity ran in to get groceries, but Ida was tired of waiting and decided she wanted to go home. She got out of the buggy, untied the horse, got back in, and headed out. She's still spry enough to do things like that, even if her mind doesn't work good anymore."

"Lucas?"

"Charity and her husband just got this new standardbred horse a week ago, and he hasn't settled in yet. Ida made him go into the wrong lane. You know how much fast traffic there is on Route 93. The oncoming cars were dodging around Ida's buggy, and a lot of them were blowing their horns. That confused her even more, and it really frightened the horse. Next thing you know, that animal was galloping down the highway completely out of control, and Ida was bouncing around inside that buggy trying to hang on."

"What's Lucas got to do with this?" I practically shouted, trying to get Erma to skip the details. "Is he okay?"

"No! He's not okay! That's what I'm trying to tell you." Erma paused for a moment, as though gathering her thoughts, and then continued. "Lucas was riding into town on that black stallion of his, and heard the car horns, and saw all the commotion and tried to do something about it. You know how good he is with horses. He probably figured his big saddle horse could catch up with Ida's buggy horse without too much trouble."

I could imagine Lucas doing exactly that.

Carolyn came back and silently took her chair.

"He caught up with the buggy horse, reached down and grabbed the harness, but the horse reared up and jerked Lucas sideways. He lost his balance and fell. Amy, Lucas fell under the buggy. He got caught on something and dragged beneath it!"

I could no longer breathe. I think my heart stopped. I jumped up from the table and shouted into the phone. "IS. LUCAS. STILL. ALIVE?"

My editor's jaw dropped. Other diners stopped eating and stared at me. A server hurried toward me. I waved him off as I headed toward the front of the hotel, Carolyn following closely behind.

"He is alive, but he's hurt bad. Internal bleeding they almost didn't find in time. A concussion—he hasn't regained consciousness yet. Three broken ribs. One of his legs is broken. He's on life support."

"Where is he now, Erma?" I asked.

"They life-flighted him to Cleveland Clinic."

I stopped moving when I got outside the hotel, trying to focus on how to get to Lucas as quickly as possible. Doormen stood about. Tourists took pictures of one another. Horns honked and traffic noisily swept by.

"I'll be there as soon as I can, Erma."

19

"You're coming to Sugarcreek?"

"Of course not. I'm going to Cleveland. Who is with him?"

"His brother-in-law, Samuel," Erma said. "Some of his sisters. His parents, Naomi and Albert."

"You forgot this." My editor shoved my purse into my hand. "We'll finish talking about your next project later."

I nodded my thanks. A taxi drove by. I waved it down.

"Where to, lady?" The driver asked.

I gave him my address. As I climbed into the taxi, the thing that struck me the strongest was how incredibly unimportant my writing career felt right now compared to the fact that doctors were fighting for Lucas's life.

Once home, I shoved clothes into a suitcase with hands that wouldn't stop shaking.

I probably shouldn't have considered driving, but there was no one around to stop me. I drove my car out of the parking garage where it lived, hit the Holland Tunnel at borderline illegal speed, and pointed my car toward Ohio.

Fields, rest stops, gas stations, barns. The highway flew past in a blur—billboards, a stalled car, road work, rain. I robotically followed my GPS while one thought throbbed continuously: Would Lucas be alive when I got there?

As I drove, my mind flew back to the morning I'd left for New York and how Lucas had brought me an armload of fresh daffodils from down near the creek. I'd gotten flowers from men before, but his had been the sweetest gesture. He knew he'd hurt me, and we both knew he had no choice.

I pressed harder on the gas.

CHAPTER 2

S even hours later, I arrived at the Cleveland Clinic. It wasn't like any hospital I'd ever known. It was like a city within a city made up of hospital buildings. I did not know where to go, how to park, or what to do. I knew there was a strong possibility that he'd been admitted to a hospital room by now—I went to the Main Entrance first.

I pulled into the roundabout, handed my car keys to the valet parking attendant, grabbed the tote bag in which I carried my life around with me, and left my other luggage behind in the car.

If Erma owned a cell phone, I could have gotten more up-to-date information from her, but I'd left half a dozen messages on the answering machine in her phone shanty, and she had not called me back.

As I headed into the hospital, I barely recognized myself in the image I saw reflected in the glass doors. I'd been a reasonably well-put-together young woman when this day had started. Now, my hair was wild, my linen pants wrinkled beyond hope, my white silk top looked like I'd dug it out of the laundry hamper, and my mascara was badly smudged from rubbing my eyes during the long drive.

A crazed raccoon with a mission.

I soon learned that the Cleveland Clinic has people in red coats who are there to help visitors find their way. The closest red-coated person I saw directed me to the J Lobby, where they wanted my ID, and Lucas's date of birth before I could be given a photo visitor's pass.

His birthday? I could barely remember my own most days. Then I remembered his youngest sister teasing him about being a Valentine baby by bringing him a pink heart-shaped cake for his birthday.

Finally, I was given directions on how to find the Neuro ICU waiting room. When I arrived, it was filled with somber-looking Amish people. Black bonnets, black hats, silent prayers and folded hands. These were people used to accepting God's will and His timing, and it showed in how they waited—not fidgeting or complaining. They politely shifted over to make room for me to sit among them.

I wondered how many *Englisch* drivers of vans and non-Amish neighbors with cars were needed to bring all these people here.

"Amy," Erma made her way to me. "I'm so glad you arrived safely!"

We were not used to hugging one another, but we hugged now and when we broke apart, both of us were fighting tears.

"How is he, Erma?"

They've put him into a medically induced coma for now while trying to get the swelling of his brain to stop. The doctor says brain injuries are unpredictable. The next twenty-four hours are critical."

I nodded, unable to trust my voice.

"His family is taking turns sitting with him. Only immediate family may go in."

"I understand."

Samuel, Lucas's brother-in-law, brought me a cup of coffee. I didn't know him well, and I couldn't have cared less about the coffee, but I was grateful for his thoughtfulness.

"Is Gretchen here?" I knew that of Lucas's five sisters, he was closest to Samuel's wife.

"She's been having trouble with her ankles swelling," he said. "The midwife thought it would be unwise for her to come. She was lying abed when I left—my *Mamm* is caring for her."

"I'm so sorry she's having problems. I hope the baby gets here safely."

"*Gott's wille*," he said.

I'd lived among the Amish long enough to know that the phrase "God's will" covered everything from birth to death and anything that might happen in between. God's will, no matter what happened, was to be accepted without complaint.

Hours passed. Amish families whispered, slept in hard hospital chairs, and shared food they had brought from home. I recognized Lucas's sisters from when I'd lived in Sugarcreek before—Martha with her organized efficiency, Regina directing traffic like a general, Susan making sure everyone had something to eat. Ellen, the youngest, who still lived at home with their parents, tried to be cheerful and keep everyone's spirits up.

The waiting room continued to fill as darkness came and word spread. Every few minutes, someone new arrived—women in plain dresses with identical prayer *kapps* pinned neatly to their hair, bearded men in broad fall trousers and suspenders.

I'd claimed a chair when I arrived, but as the night deepened, my presence felt increasingly intrusive. I was taking up space from people who had an actual right to be here—people connected to Lucas by blood or faith. The familiar feeling of existing in the margins crept back.

My seat was close to the door, and I gave it up to an elderly Amish woman who seemed especially frail. I brought her a bottle of water and stayed with her until her driver, who turned out to be her *Englisch* son, joined her after parking the car. People shifted around so that he could sit next to his mother. I retreated to a far corner of the room because there were no remaining seats. There was an outlet in that corner, so I plugged in my laptop and phone to recharge. Then I slid down to sit on the floor with my back against the wall, hugging my knees, trying not to be in anyone's way.

Hours passed. Whispered Pennsylvania Dutch conversations ebbed and flowed around me like water around a stone. The steady beeping of monitors drifted through each time the doors to the patient area opened.

Some tried to sleep, heads tilted at uncomfortable angles against the wall or on a neighbor's shoulder. No one complained about the wait. Their stoic acceptance of this uncomfortable situation struck me as remarkable.

I studied them, these people who had shaped Lucas into the man I knew. There was something solid about them, an unshakeable foundation that I envied. In New York, I'd prided myself on my independence, my ability to thrive without relying on anyone. But watching this community rally around one of their own made me wonder if I'd mistaken the ability to normalize loneliness for strength.

I dozed fitfully on the floor, eventually curling up and shoving the tote I used as a combination purse and laptop carrier beneath my head as a makeshift pillow. The parade of squeaking nursing shoes passing in the hallway woke me often.

Dawn arrived without fanfare, gray light seeping into the waiting room as if apologizing for its intrusion. With it came Lucas's father from beyond the double doors—his face gray and drawn with exhaustion and worry.

"Lucas has made it through the night," Albert gratefully announced. "His heartbeat is strong, but the swelling of his brain continues to worry them."

Murmurs ran through the room. Lucas's father raised his hand, silencing them.

"Whatever happens, we will pray, and we will accept God's will."

The simplicity of his faith, stated without qualification or doubt, gave me chills. In my world, such certainty seemed naïve. But here, surrounded by these people who had built their lives on unwavering belief, it felt like the most practical thing in the world.

An elderly man pulled a Bible from his coat pocket. He opened it without ceremony and read aloud in German. Some people closed their eyes, and let the words sink in, the weariness on their faces transformed into something more serene. No one seemed embarrassed by this public display of faith. Here, in this place of crisis, prayer and scripture felt as natural as breathing.

I watched, both drawn to and separated from their ritual. The cynic in me wanted to dismiss it as nothing more than superstition. But something deeper in me yearned for their certainty.

When I was a child, my mother hadn't exactly prioritized church attendance, but when I was ten, we lived in an apartment in LA next to a church advertising Vacation Bible School. Mom saw it as an opportunity for free babysitting.

I was entranced. I loved the little Bible classes, the crafts, the cookies, the songs. I loved the kind faces of the teachers. Then we moved farther across town, and I never went again. Watching this room filled with Amish, I wondered if God took the prayers of a people with such unquestioning faith more seriously than others?

As an adult, my entire religious experience boiled down to a few visits to St. Patrick's Cathedral in New York City, just because I enjoyed sitting in the beautiful sanctuary. It gave me a measure of peace in the middle of the frantic bustle of the city. With a religious background that shallow, if there was a God—and I was fairly certain there was—I did not think He would take my desperate, inarticulate pleas seriously.

But sitting there in my wrinkled clothes, surrounded by people who could trace their lineage back through generations of shared belief, I wished I knew more. I wished I had the right to pray for Lucas and be heard.

No, that's a lie. I didn't really want to pray. Nothing so tame. What

I wanted to do was scream and cry and pound the floor with my fists and beg for Lucas's life.

Instead, I kept it buried inside. I sat and watched the morning sun stretch golden fingers across the parking lot. Another day had begun, oblivious to the desperation inside these walls, where time felt suspended.

I pressed the heels of my hands against my eyes, fighting back the flood of tears that I knew I could not let start. If I did, I feared they'd wash away whatever glue that had been holding me together so far. It was one thing to sit vigil with the others. I was his friend and employer and therefore had understandable concern. Being there was to show my respect for what the family was going through. But if I allowed Lucas's people to see how deeply this was affecting me, they would assume there had been a lot more involved in our relationship than there was.

Because I was *Englisch* they felt no obligation to monitor my morality or lack of it. But Lucas? If that poor man ever woke up from his head injury, I didn't want him to discover he'd been shunned because I'd fallen apart and started wailing in the waiting room. The constant calibration of appropriate emotional responses was exhausting.

I tried calling my mother to tell her where I was and what had happened, but she was on location for yet another movie, and my message went to voicemail. Not a surprise. In a crisis, some people could count on their mothers to drop everything and rush to their side. Sadly, that had never been the case for me. My relationship with my mother, Desiree Stanton, was complicated.

I tried to doze, but that was impossible, so I went for a walk in the hospital corridors. My body ached from lying on the hard floor, and I remembered seeing seats in the main lobby. This early in the morning, there were several vacant. Gratefully, I sank into one, closed my eyes and attempted to pray. Here in this echoing lobby, there was no one close by to hear me.

"Please don't let him die," I whispered. "Lucas is such a good man. Please let him live."

The words came out ungracefully. I wasn't good at begging for favors—not even from invisible forces. I was more of a do-it-yourself kind of person.

So, I bargained.

"If he lives and is okay, I'll let go. I promise. I'll accept it even if he marries someone else. Just let him get well."

I meant it. These past hours had taught me that Lucas marrying some other woman was not the worst thing that could happen. Losing him completely was worse. Right now, I would happily, joyfully, *enthusiastically* embrace any woman he chose if it meant him being well and strong again. I just wanted him to be okay. That had become my greatest, most heartfelt desire.

I sat there for quite a while with my head leaning back against the back of the seat. It was definitely more comfortable than the floor of the waiting room. Then a stocky, middle-aged Amish man I'd never met walked into the corner where I sat.

"Please forgive the interruption," he said. "I'm a friend of Lucas. I saw you in the waiting room tonight. You didn't come back. Are you okay?"

"I am." I sat up. "I've just been trying to pray, but I think I'm doing it wrong."

"I think you are probably doing just fine." He took a seat across from me. "I'm Bishop Noah Schrock, by the way."

"I'm Amy Stanton—I own the farm where Lucas works."

"I know. You are Erma's friend. She's mentioned you to me."

I didn't know whether that was good or bad. I couldn't imagine what Erma might have told him, but I could tell this wasn't the bishop I'd heard Lucas talk about.

"I thought Elmer Yoder was the bishop," I said.

"Elmer died two months ago. He was ninety-five. Did you know him?" Bishop Noah asked.

"No, but I heard about how he shunned Lucas for a period for questioning your rules. It seemed very unfair." If I had been rested, I might not have said such a disrespectful thing—but lack of sleep had removed my filters. I was too tired and upset to care much about what I said.

Something flickered across Bishop Noah's face—an expression of sadness mixed with relief. "Bishop Elmer wanted to be a good leader." He paused. "But he believed in leading with a firm hand. Some might say too firm."

The careful diplomacy in his voice told me he understood exactly why I might have negative feelings about the former bishop.

"I'm sorry for your church's loss." I meant it despite my prejudice against a man who had felt it necessary to discipline Lucas.

"Danki." Noah's eyes were gentle as he looked at me. There was no judgment in them, which was something I found remarkable in an Amish bishop. "Lucas has spoken to me of the difficulties he faced under Bishop Elmer's leadership. I'm sorry he went through that. I've always believed young men need room to grow in their faith, not simply follow without understanding. We have had some interesting talks—Lucas and I—since I became bishop. I've enjoyed them."

The contrast between this man's compassion and the rigid authoritarianism that had been the earmark of Bishop Yoder's leadership was striking. I filed away details—the way Noah spoke about his predecessor with respect but obvious disagreement, the way he avoided direct criticism while making his position clear.

He rose with the same quiet dignity he'd shown when he arrived.

"I thought you might want to know that Lucas's father has told the hospital staff that as far as visitation goes, you are to be treated as immediate family."

"Seriously?" I was surprised. "Why?"

"Word spread tonight when our people saw you give up your seat and help care for old Jane Yoder. Kindness carries weight with our people."

"I did very little."

"Lucas's sister, Martha, was the one who pointed it out," he continued. "She said any woman who'd sit on a hospital floor all night to make room for others deserved to be treated like family. Regina agreed with her—and when Regina agrees with something, the rest of the Hershberger family tend to fall in line."

I did not know Lucas's family well. They had not been allowed to have anything to do with Lucas during most of the short time I'd lived in Sugarcreek because Bishop Elmer had punished Lucas for his "rebellious spirit" by exacting six months of shunning.

"The doctors have said that family presence can aid recovery. You and Lucas were good friends. The family thinks that the sound of your voice might be helpful. I thought you'd want to know."

Bishop Noah left me feeling better than before he'd arrived. Apparently, I was going to be allowed to see Lucas after all—and that was an unexpected gift. I gathered up my things and followed him into the elevator.

CHAPTER 3

W hen I returned to the waiting room, Lucas's father, Albert, took me to see Lucas. He led me past rooms that were each its own private universe of misery and hope. Some had families keeping vigil, others had only the patient inside. When we reached Lucas's alcove in the neuro ICU, I thought I was ready.

I wasn't. Nothing could have prepared me for seeing him diminished like this.

The Lucas I knew was built as though he could lift his end of a barn and could command respect by his mere presence, without even raising his voice. He was, in my eyes at least, bigger than life.

The man lying in the bed looked impossibly small amid the tangle of tubes and wires, as if the accident had stolen not just his strength but his very substance.

They'd shaved his beard and hair for surgery. Bandages covered part of his face and skull, and without the familiar frame of dark hair and beard, he looked like a stranger. The purple and black bruises blooming across his skin were stark against a pallor that spoke of blood loss and trauma.

His left leg was elevated and in a cast. Bandages wrapped his chest tightly—broken ribs, Albert explained, one of which had nearly punctured a lung.

I had expected Albert to leave me alone with him, but he stayed. Under the circumstances, I was grateful for his presence. It was a frightening place to be.

The rhythmic hiss of the ventilator marked time like a metronome, each mechanical breath a reminder of how close he'd come to eternal silence. Numbers on the screens changed constantly—heart rate, blood pressure, oxygen levels—reducing this man I cared about to data points and digital readouts.

A nurse was checking his IV when we entered. She looked up with the practiced compassion of someone who shepherded families through this particular hell daily.

"Ten minutes," she said, noticing that this was my first visit. "Please don't touch any equipment. Talk normally—hearing is often preserved even when there's no other response."

The words hung in the sterile air as she left us alone with the machines and their symphony of survival.

"Lucas," I whispered, then cleared my throat and tried again with more force. "Lucas, it's Amy." There really was no reason to whisper.

Nothing changed. No flicker of awareness behind closed eyelids, no shift in the mechanical rise and fall of his chest. The ventilator continued its work, indifferent to my presence or to my breaking heart.

"I'm so sorry you got hurt." The words felt pathetically inadequate for the magnitude of what lay before me.

I looked around the clinical space, taking in monitors that never stopped calculating, bags of clear fluid hanging like transparent fruit from metal trees, and the chair positioned for visitors to sit and wait and hope.

On the bedside table, someone had left a copy of the 23rd Psalm. Aside from a few Bible stories like Noah's Ark, it was the only scripture with which I had any familiarity. A college literary professor had read it once as an example of Hebrew poetry. I grabbed it and began to read aloud, my voice gaining strength as ancient poetry filled the space between us.

"The Lord is my shepherd; I shall not want. He maketh me to lie down in green pastures: he leadeth me beside the still waters."

The words seemed to push back against the clinical precision of medical technology while Albert stood near the door, allowing me a few feet of privacy. But whether anyone was listening felt irrelevant. Reading those verses became an act of defiance against my own despair.

"Yea, though I walk through the valley of the shadow of death, I will fear no evil: for thou art with me; thy rod and thy staff they comfort me."

His hand lay pale and still against the white blanket. I covered it with mine, startled by how cold his skin felt, how fragile the bones seemed beneath the translucent flesh.

"Come back," I said, abandoning the psalm for words that came from my heart. "Your family needs you. The farm needs you."

With Albert standing there, I didn't add what I wanted to say, at least not out loud, but in my heart, I said, "And I need you, Lucas. More than I ever dreamed possible."

A soft chime from one of the monitors interrupted me—nothing alarming, just the machine documenting another moment of Lucas's tenuous hold on life. I squeezed his hand gently, imagining pressure in return, knowing it was nothing but wishful thinking but choosing to hope, anyway.

When the nurse returned to signal my time was up, I didn't argue. The rest of his family longed for their time with him too—time to whisper their own prayers and promises over him. I was grateful for the few minutes I'd been given. But walking away from that bed felt like leaving a part of myself behind.

The following hours blurred together in hospital coffee and too few medical updates.

Lucas remained unconscious.

CHAPTER 4

I spent the next morning and afternoon alternately waiting in the waiting room and sitting beside Lucas's hospital bed, grateful his family continued to let me take part. I think it was a risk for them, and for him, to allow this—there had to be talk among his people about what this *Englisch* woman from New York City was doing there among them—but his sisters seemed to have things under control. Martha and Regina were apparently a force in the Amish community.

Erma confided that this family leniency was mainly because his five sisters had worried continuously over him after his wife died. He'd trudged through his work, doing what had to be done, but was no longer the cheerful brother they had known. After I moved to the farm, they'd noticed positive changes in him—laughter for one thing, where there had been none before. Now that he was so damaged, they hoped the sound of my voice might help bring him back. I hoped that was true, but there were no miraculous recoveries. Each minute I spent beside his hospital bed was no different from the last.

Eventually, the doctors successfully removed the ventilator, and Lucas breathed on his own—a milestone that felt monumental after watching machines do that work for him. But consciousness remained elusive, as if his mind was taking longer to heal than the rest of his body.

Illness can have an odd effect on those who must sit and watch. I had never been a superstitious person. Even as a little girl, I'd never worried about stepping on a crack and breaking my mother's back or any of the other silly things I heard from other children or adults.

I think it was the feeling of utter powerlessness that overcame my common sense and translated into a need to do something, *anything*, that might bring Lucas back. I had read the 23rd Psalm out loud to him until I had memorized it, and I longed for something more. Even though I was certain that there was no lack of Bibles in that hospital, I fixated on wanting Lucas's personal Bible—the one I'd seen in his hands every evening that I'd lived on the farm. My mind knew that there was no magic in one print copy over another, but my heart wanted *his*—the one with the gray duct tape holding the spine together after so many years of use.

With the decision made, I mentioned to Erma that I was going to drive to the farm to get Lucas's Bible. I didn't want her worrying about me if she noticed I was gone.

"*Ach*, I need to go home, too!" Erma said. "Sleeping in a chair is not good for old bones. And I should check on my chickens. I know they're free range, but they need a little chicken feed to supplement their diet, and I've been worried about whether their watering device is working. Do you mind?"

"Of course not. I'd be happy for the company."

I wasn't surprised by the request. In Amish culture, necessity expands to fill whatever transportation presents itself.

"I should go home and check on Gretchen," Samuel added, materializing beside us. "Her swollen ankles are worrying me."

Within moments, what had begun as a simple errand to retrieve a Bible—had been transformed into a logistical operation. Two other Amish men I barely knew asked if they could ride along. Had I been driving a fifteen-passenger van, I think I could have filled it.

I couldn't refuse, and I didn't want to. These people had been nothing but kind to me, and their own lives were also being disrupted by this crisis. Besides, the thought of making the drive alone, with nothing but my own spiraling thoughts for company, was not something I looked forward to.

As soon as I got the five of us packed into my car and navigated out of Cleveland onto the highway, I asked what I thought was a simple question. "What chores will need to be handled on the farm while Lucas is recovering?"

What followed was a tutorial in rural reality that made my head spin.

The massive Belgian workhorses, King and Prince, needed daily exercise or they'd go stir-crazy and start kicking their stalls apart. The vegetable garden required constant attention—hoeing, watering, and vigilance against an army of insects.

The cattle needed to be moved to fresh pasture every few days, the chicken coop required cleaning (with warnings about wearing a mask to avoid histoplasmosis—a disease they assured me I did *not* want to contract), and Lucas had been planning to harvest the hay this week because rain was predicted soon.

"And that's just the most urgent stuff," Erma added helpfully from the passenger seat. "He mentioned to me last week that there's a fence needing repair in the north field, and the barn roof has a leak that needs attention before winter, plus he's got orders for your organic garden produce he needs to deliver to three different restaurants in the area in a couple more days."

Samuel nodded gravely. "Lucas got behind on things at your place during my absence in the spring. He was managing both his work and mine. I'm sorry for that."

Even now, months after his return, guilt colored his voice when he spoke of the time he'd disappeared, leaving his family and responsibilities without explanation.

"But the church will help," one man in the back seat assured me.

37

"Bishop Noah is already organizing work parties. We take care of our own."

The phrase stuck with me. We take care of our own. In New York, "our own" usually meant whoever you were currently dating or your immediate family if you were lucky enough to have one. The idea of a community that functioned as an extended family, that showed up without being asked, was foreign to me. Foreign and appealing.

Here, it seemed to encompass anyone who needed help, whether they were born Amish or simply an *Englisch* neighbor.

"Do you mind stopping at the IGA before you take me home?" Erma asked as we approached Sugarcreek.

"Of course I don't mind," I said, despite realizing this simple trip home could take considerably longer than expected.

It turned out that Erma wasn't the only one with sudden shopping needs. Free transportation, it seemed, was not to be underutilized. As we pulled into the grocery store parking lot, I watched all four of my passengers produce lists that had materialized during the drive.

"Just a few things for the girls," Samuel said apologetically. "Since I'm already here."

"Won't take but a minute," promised one of the other men, already heading for the store entrance with the determined stride of someone I suspected would need much more than a minute.

I waited in the car, fighting exhaustion. The afternoon sun beat through the windshield, and the emotional toll of the past thirty-six hours descended over me like a heavy blanket. By the time everyone had made their purchases and returned to the car, I had fallen asleep.

After waking up and dropping everyone at their respective homes, each stop accompanied by thanks and gentle pats on my shoulder that somehow made me want to cry, I finally pulled into my driveway.

Coming home should have brought comfort, but instead I felt a hollow ache that nearly overwhelmed me. The farm looked exactly as it had when I'd left four months earlier, yet everything felt wrong.

Empty. Lucas's absence had transformed these familiar spaces into painful reminders of what I might lose forever.

And yet, I had chores to do. Animals to be fed. Eggs to gather. I couldn't allow the farm to fall apart. If he survived, I wanted him to have something to come home to.

Then I noticed two Amish boys, probably fifteen or sixteen. One was inside the chicken yard with the egg basket on his arm, moving with the mastery of someone who wasn't bothered by Zedekiah's particular brand of poultry terrorism.

"Jacob Yoder," the boy introduced himself as I walked over to the chicken fence. "I'm Ben Yoder's boy. That's my cousin, Jacob Mast."

He pointed at another Amish boy, hoeing weeds in Lucas's enormous vegetable garden with the methodical precision of someone who knew exactly what he was doing.

"*Daett* sent us to keep things going around here until Lucas returns."

"My goodness!" I felt my load of worry lighten. "He sent both of you?"

This was a major gift. Amish teenagers were respected for their work ethic and skill. These boys, no doubt, had a much better grasp of what needed to be done than I did.

"*Ja*," Jacob said. "We both live just down the road. It is no problem for us to come help. And *Daett* comes by every morning to check our work and tell us what needs doing. The bishop organized others who will tend to the haying, fence repair, and cattle."

I reached for my purse. "I want to pay you for your help."

"*Daett* says that is not allowed." Jacob took a step back. "Lucas helped for many weeks when *Daett* was sick with pneumonia. We were too small to be any help. *Mamm* was pregnant with Lucy. We will not take pay for returning Lucas's kindness."

My throat burned with the effort of not breaking down in front of this earnest boy. These people, whose rigid orthodoxy had once felt so incomprehensible, had already mobilized to protect the farm into which Lucas had poured the past several years of his life.

I choked out a "thank you."

After checking that the boys had everything they needed, I walked toward the *Daadi Haus,* where Lucas, as farm manager, lived. I steeled myself to enter. I'd only been inside twice, and both times for specific, practical reasons. Even though I legally owned the property, stepping inside felt like a violation.

I swung the door open to reveal the spare, neat interior I remembered. Everything exactly where it should be. Dishes washed and put away, woodstove cold but ready to light, the rocking chair positioned by the window where I'd often seen his silhouette in the evenings as he read by lamplight. Although my larger farmhouse had electricity, his home did not. His refrigerator was propane powered; his bathroom and kitchen water were gravity-fed. Lucas was not one to break his church's rules.

Sparse but solid furniture, each piece functional rather than decorative. The kitchen contained exactly what was necessary for survival, nothing more. No photographs adorned the walls, no mementos spoke of sentiment. Only the large wall calendar with its careful penciled notations hinted at the methodical mind that governed this space and ran this farm. The rooms held a peculiar emptiness of a life paused mid-sentence.

His Bible sat on the small table beside his rocking chair. It was nearly falling apart from years of daily use. He'd used duct tape to hold the spine together instead of purchasing a new one. The rest of the cover was rubbed velvety soft from handling. The margins were covered with penciled notes.

I opened it expecting old German, but instead, English words flowed before me as I thumbed through the pages.

In the book of Job, I read: *"But he knows the way that I take; when he has tested me, I will come forth as gold."*

Lucas's precise handwriting filled the margins beside it. Not just references, but conversations with scripture. Each notation was a window into struggles he'd never shared with me, his faith tested and refined in silence.

"Remembered this verse when the corn failed, 2018."

I flipped through more pages, hungry to see what he'd written, craving a small window into his mind.

From the 34th Psalm:

"The Lord is close to the brokenhearted and saves those who are crushed in spirit."

He'd written beneath: *"The Lord was my only comfort after Rebecca died."*

I flipped through more pages, finding passage after passage marked with careful pencil strokes, many accompanied by Lucas's commentary. The man didn't just read the Bible, he absorbed it.

And then I found the entry that stopped my breath:

"I pray for Amy's safety in New York. Lord, please bring her home."

The notation was dated just two weeks earlier.

That's when the dam I'd built around my emotions burst.

I sank into Lucas's rocking chair, clutching his Bible to my chest, and let all the pain and fear I'd been holding back since Erma's phone call spill out.

Great, gulping, primal sobs. All the tears I'd fought back for his sake came pouring out into the sanctuary of his home. I cried until my chest ached and my eyes burned, until I could barely breathe and there was nothing left but the hiccupping aftermath of emotional exhaustion.

When the storm passed, I sat in his chair, surrounded by a profound silence. The late afternoon sun slanted through his windows, illuminating dust motes that danced in the golden light, and for the first time since this nightmare began, I felt something that resembled peace. Or maybe it was just the strange, washed-out calm that comes after one has cried every tear a human body can produce.

41

CHAPTER 5

I was hunting for a tissue when my eyes fell on something lying on the table beside Lucas's chair. The item hadn't registered with me earlier—an old bridle Lucas had apparently been working on before his accident. A soft polishing cloth and a small jar of Wright's Silver Cream sat nearby.

Lucas's hands were rarely still. If he wasn't repairing farming equipment, he was fixing a toy one of his nephews or nieces brought to him. They seemed confident that their uncle could fix anything— and he usually did.

Now, with Lucas's life hanging by a thread, it suddenly became terribly important to me to finish this small task he'd laid aside. Maybe it was just more superstition, maybe it was my desperate need to do something that connected me to him, but after blowing my nose and mopping up my tears, I picked up the polishing cloth in one hand and the bridle in the other and set out to complete the job Lucas had begun.

I was no expert, but the bridle appeared to be of unusually high quality. The leather was beautiful and crafted with close attention to the stitching. It had real silver fittings, many of which already gleamed from Lucas's careful work. But several pieces remained tarnished, including a medallion about the size of a silver dollar positioned to rest on a horse's forehead.

As I worked, the repetitive motion soothed my raw nerves. The smaller pieces cleaned easily, revealing intricate craftsmanship that spoke of Old-World skill. I noticed what I assumed was a name stamped into the leatherwork on the side of the bridle. It was small; I hadn't noticed it at first. It said, "Stute Sokora." I assumed that was the name of the horse that had worn it. The words meant nothing to me. Horses were given strange names all the time.

I saved the medallion for last. There appeared to be some sort of etching beneath the tarnish. It looked like it might be a bird of some kind.

I dipped the cloth in silver cream and set to work. At first, I thought I was seeing a stylized eagle emerging from beneath decades of neglect as I continued to rub.

My hands were getting tired by that point, but I kept on because I wanted to finish, and I was curious about the etching. As more of the image became visible, I realized the eagle was clutching something in its talons. I worked more carefully, curious about what decorative element would complete the design.

When the last of the tarnish cleared away, I stared at something in my hands that made me nauseous: a swastika, stark and unmistakable, was etched into the medallion's polished surface.

The discovery was so unexpected, I shoved the bridle from my lap. Silver fittings chimed against each other like discordant bells as it fell to the floor.

There was no mistake. This was a Nazi bridle—or meant to look like one. How could it have ended up here, at Lucas's home? He was certainly no Nazi. How could it be here in Sugarcreek among all these gentle people who had for centuries made pacifism one of their religious cornerstones?

Could this be something that had belonged to Rick? My stepfather had been an appraiser for Sotheby's—someone who dealt in artifacts from all over the world, including pieces with dark histories. Was it possible this bridle had come from his collection? The questions multiplied in my mind.

Back in the main house, I showered away layers of fear, sweat, and grime, letting the hot water wash away everything I couldn't control.

Lucas's Bible sat on my nightstand, a comforting presence.

Hunger drove me to the kitchen, where I discovered Erma had been busy during my absence. The freezer was stocked with neatly labeled containers in her precise handwriting: "Chicken Casserole - June 24." "Beef Stew - July 8." "Tuna Noodle - July 12."

Like Rick before me, I'd hired her to come once a week to clean. Apparently, she'd taken it upon herself also to fill my freezer with home-cooked meals—bless her.

She must have suspected I'd come back.

I warmed the beef stew, grateful beyond words for Erma's practical kindness.

The microwave dinged, telling me that Erma's stew was ready. The insignia I'd discovered etched onto the bridle's medallion continued to bother me. I set the container on the kitchen table to cool while I opened my laptop. It wouldn't hurt, I thought, if I did a quick bit of research while I waited for my bowl of stew to cool.

I typed "Nazi horse's bridle" into the search bar and started digging. The results were a strange mix of historical auction listings, museum collections, and scholarly articles on Nazi appropriation of horse breeding programs. Page after page confirmed what I'd suspected—the bridle was likely from the 1930s or 1940s, possibly used by mounted SS officers or cavalry units.

Some of the fancier examples had been presentation pieces, given to high-ranking officials rather than used in actual service. Others had been working bridles, designed for controlling animals trained for war. All of them were worth money to collectors—some of whom had questionable taste and flexible morals.

But nothing explained how such an object would have made its way to Sugarcreek, much less into Lucas's possession. The Amish had been pacifists for centuries, conscientious objectors who refused military service on religious grounds. Many had faced persecution during both world wars for their stance. Finding Nazi regalia in an Amish home was like discovering a strip club in a convent—theoretically possible but highly unlikely.

I closed the laptop, more confused than when I'd started. The bridle was incompatible with everything I knew about Lucas and the Sugarcreek community. With my eyes refusing to focus, I crawled into bed and slept for nine hours straight.

CHAPTER 6

The next day, I was waiting for my turn to see Lucas, when a commotion near the elevator jolted me awake. A tall, broad-shouldered man in a cowboy hat was speaking urgently to a nurse, his weathered face creased with worry.

"Brady?" I stood up, not quite believing my eyes.

My father, a seasoned bullfighter, whose job it was to help protect young rodeo bull riders when they got thrown, turned and enveloped me in a bear hug that smelled of leather, aftershave, and rodeo dust. Few hugs had ever felt so good.

"Why didn't you call me?" He sounded like I'd hurt his feelings.

I told him the truth. "I didn't know if you'd want me to."

"What do you mean, you didn't know if I'd want you to! Of course I did!" My dad suddenly remembered he was wearing his cowboy hat inside a building and politely removed it.

"I'm not sure how this is supposed to work, Brady. We met each other for the first time only four months ago."

He glanced around, as though looking for someone. "Is your mother here for you, at least?"

"She's on location—in Romania, I think. I'm not sure." I walked toward the waiting room seats with Brady following me.

"You aren't sure?"

The disgust in his voice made me wince. Desiree Stanton was not on Brady's list of favorite people. Not since she'd walked out of their marriage without letting him know she was leaving or that they were going to have a daughter.

"How did you find out I was here?" We sat down, and I turned in my seat to face him. I still could hardly believe my actual father was sitting there with me. I'd been so long without knowing I even had a father.

"I was working at a rodeo up near Burbank, Ohio, and the news made it onto the local radio station. 'Lucas Hershberger. Amish. Injured while trying to stop a runaway buggy.' Called you, but there was no answer. Checked around and found out where they'd taken him. I figured you'd be here, too."

I checked my phone. Sure enough, I'd turned it off during my vigil in the waiting room. I hadn't wanted it to bother the Amish people seated around me. It hadn't occurred to me to turn it back on. "Sorry about the phone. You really didn't have to come. I'm okay."

"Look, I've never had a daughter before. I don't know how this is supposed to work either." Brady rubbed the back of his neck. "It's your choice. But I spent twenty-nine years missing everything that mattered to you. Unless you tell me to leave, I'm not going anywhere until that boy of yours is out of the woods."

I didn't know what Lucas would think of being called "that boy" of mine, but I knew in my dad's cowboy vernacular, it was probably a term of endearment.

"I'd really like it if you could stay, Brady."

He smiled. "That's all I needed to hear."

CHAPTER 7

Nine days after the accident, Brady had moved his RV to the farm and was helping there. I was again reading out loud to Lucas from his Bible, specifically focusing on the various passages he'd underlined. They'd taken him off the meds that had kept him in the coma. I kept hoping the verses would trigger something profound enough in his brain that he would awaken.

As I carefully turned one of those delicately thin pages, I glanced up and saw the faintest flutter of his eyelids.

"Did you see that?" I asked the nurse, who'd just entered.

"See what?" She leaned over him, her trained eyes searching for signs I'd probably imagined.

"I think his eyelids moved. Like he was trying to open them."

She watched intently. "Mr. Hershberger? Lucas? Can you hear me?"

Nothing.

"It might have been an involuntary muscle spasm," she said, delivering hope and caution in equal measure. "With brain injuries, sometimes the body does things that seem meaningful but aren't conscious responses."

"But could it have been real?"

"It could have been. Keep talking to him. If he's surfacing, familiar voices will help guide him back."

So, I kept reading, kept talking, maintained my one-sided conversation with a man who might or might not be listening. I told him about the Amish boys who were helping back at the farm, about how the late tomatoes were coming in beautifully, about Zedekiah's continued territorial attitude.

"That bird struts around like he owns the place," I said, warming to the subject. "You're going to have to have a serious talk with him when you get home."

Was that another flutter? This time I knew I saw definite movement behind closed lids, as if he was fighting to wake up.

Two hours later, I was again taking my turn in his room, when I heard a soft, rasping voice.

"Thirsty." The word was slurred, barely recognizable. My eyes flew to his face. Lucas was looking at me through half-closed lids, his gaze unfocused but trying to track movement.

"Lucas?" I whispered, afraid that speaking too loudly might break whatever fragile connection was forming.

He blinked slowly, his brow furrowing with the effort of concentration.

"Water," he managed, the word thick and unclear.

I nearly knocked over my chair reaching for the call button. Within moments, the room filled with medical staff—Dr. Peterson with her dignified authority, nurses moving with practiced efficiency, checking monitors and responses.

"Mr. Hershberger, do you know where you are?" Dr. Peterson asked, shining a small light in his eyes.

Lucas's gaze drifted around the room, taking in the equipment, the white walls, and the concerned faces surrounding his bed. The effort of focusing seemed to exhaust him.

A long pause. "Hospital," he said finally, each syllable requiring effort.

"That's right. Do you know what day it is?"

Another long pause. I could see him struggling to form a word. "M-Midnight?"

"No, Mr. Hershberger," the doctor said. "The sun is out. It is nearly noon."

"That's not what he's saying." I interrupted the doctor. "That's his horse's name. The horse he was riding when he got hurt. Midnight. He loves that horse."

"Midnight didn't get hurt, Lucas," I assured him. "Midnight is just fine."

Lucas's eyes found mine again, and I saw recognition there—not just of my face, but of what my presence meant.

"Amy." Wonder threaded through his voice as he said my name. He closed his eyes, exhausted from the effort of saying the four most precious words I had ever heard uttered.

The way he'd said my name—as if my being there was the most miraculous thing imaginable—nearly brought on another crying episode, but I fought it back.

The medical team continued their examination, testing his responses, checking coordination, asking questions about pain levels and memory.

"He asked for water," I reminded them.

A nurse brought a cup of water with a straw, but he couldn't manage it. She switched to a sponge swab soaked in water, which helped ease his thirst.

After that, he could give a few more one-word answers—each evidence that Lucas Hershberger was still in there, fighting his way back to us.

When they finished, Dr. Peterson wore the first genuine smile I'd seen from her.

"This is exceptional progress," she said. That he's oriented, recognizes you, remembers basic facts—it's very encouraging. We'll continue monitoring, but this is exactly what we'd hoped to see. I'll go let his family know."

While I waited for his family to come, I continued to talk to him, reassuring him again that his horse was fine, the old woman in the runaway buggy unharmed, and the farm in good hands.

"People from your church are taking care of everything while you get better. Bishop Noah created a schedule. Brady is there helping, too. There's nothing for you to worry about except concentrating on getting better."

He drifted back to sleep as I sat with him, listening to the steady beep of monitors that now sounded like music instead of warnings. He was back. Damaged, diminished, facing a long road to recovery—but back.

Over the next two days, Lucas drifted in and out of awareness. Sometimes he knew me, sometimes he stared blankly when I spoke. Sometimes he lapsed into Pennsylvania Dutch, and I'd run for someone from his family to translate. The headaches were severe—any light made him wince and close his eyes. He'd try to follow conversations but lose the thread halfway through.

"It's normal," Dr. Peterson assured me. "Brain injuries heal in waves, not straight lines. But he's progressing faster than our usual timeline. That Amish work ethic seems to extend to his healing process."

When I told Erma what the doctor had said, she looked up from her knitting. "Amish work ethic? That's not what's happening. *Der Herr* is giving him strength. Plain and simple."

"*Der Herr*?"

She glanced toward the ceiling. "The Father."

I did not argue with her. I remembered my promise—my middle-of-the-night-in-the-hospital-lobby-prayer. If Lucas made a full recovery, I had made a bargain I intended to keep. It wouldn't be easy, but things of value seldom were.

CHAPTER 8

A my dad's insistence, I rented a room at a local hotel within walking distance of the hospital. Since I only used it to shower and catch a few hours' sleep each night, I also offered it for Lucas's sisters and mother to use whenever they needed to rest or to bathe.

We weren't always all at the hospital at the same time. His sisters took turns going home to care for one another's children. But overall, staying with Lucas had become a team effort. Now that he was no longer in the ICU, the hospital was lenient with visitation hours, and the Amish seldom let anyone struggling with illness face it alone.

In the meantime, I found Lucas's sisters and mother to be delightful companions. I especially enjoyed Ellen, the youngest. She had a mischievous sense of humor and obviously adored her big brother.

"I can hardly wait for Lucas to get well enough to tease him again," Ellen said one day. "Being nice to him all the time is getting on my nerves."

Once Lucas's status was downgraded, and we knew he would live, Albert went back to Sugarcreek and his job at one of the furniture stores. He came back on weekends, and the first time he came back, he did the strangest thing. He carefully sat down on the bed and uncovered Lucas's feet. Then he took a small vial of some sort of sweet-smelling oil out of his front pocket and rubbed it on the exposed skin of his son's feet.

Lucas didn't seem surprised by this, nor did Ellen. In fact, they continued conversing as though it were the most normal thing in the world. I was sitting in the corner, checking emails on my phone, so I didn't say a word. I knew a lot about Amish customs by that time, but this was not part of any tradition I'd seen before.

It was only after Albert left, when Martha and her mother took over staying with Lucas, and Ellen and I found ourselves in my hotel room getting ready for bed, that I broached the subject.

"I have to ask," I said, as I watched Ellen take her hair out of its complicated braids beneath her *kapp* and brushed it out. "So why was Albert rubbing Lucas's feet?"

"You mean *Daett's* reflexology?"

"So *that's* what it was!" I knew some people believed various illnesses could be cured by pressing and rubbing certain places on the bottoms of their feet, but I'd always thought it was bogus. "Does it work?"

Ellen laid down her brush and created one long braid to sleep in. "I don't know, but our family has been very healthy... until now, of course. *Mamm* says *Daett* got a book about it when Martha was born. Whenever any of us got a fever when we were children, or a headache or whatever, *Daett* would rub our feet. It always felt so good, we never cared if it actually worked or not—just having *Daett* do that made us feel a little better."

"And he still does?"

"Not after we grew up, no," Ellen said. "We rub our own feet when they hurt, or take an aspirin or whatever, but sometimes when the grandchildren have something wrong with them, my sisters bring them to *Daett*."

"So, your father doesn't just go around rubbing everyone's feet at random?"

"Not unless we beg him," Ellen laughed. "I'm sure it's been years for Lucas. But I guess *Daett* felt it was something he could do that might help."

"What kind of oil was he using?"

"That's called Thieves Oil. *Daett* buys it from our cousin, who is into aromatherapy. I love the smell, don't you?"

That night, as I went to sleep, I allowed myself a small fantasy—just a little one. Lucas and I were married, with a little three-year-old girl of our own. We were cozied up on the couch, watching the fire in the fireplace while Lucas gently rubbed our daughter's sweet little feet while she fell asleep, safe in her daddy's arms.

I was so tired, I dozed for a few minutes, then jerked awake—surprised to find my face wet with tears. It was going to be harder than I thought to keep my promise.

CHAPTER 9

On August sixth, three weeks after the accident, Lucas was sitting up in a gray hospital patient chair when I arrived. The worst of the bruising on Lucas's face had faded to yellowish green. A patchy beard had grown in.

"How are you feeling?"

"Like I was dragged behind a buggy." He smiled at his mild attempt at humor.

Apparently, today was going to be a good day. Yesterday, he had struggled when the doctor asked him to remember his address and had fallen asleep mid-sentence.

"The doctors say I can probably go home in a couple of weeks."

"That's wonderful!"

"Is it?"

His comment puzzled me.

"What do you mean?" I said, puzzled. "Of course it is."

"It took everything I had to keep the farm profitable when I was healthy. I may go home, but I'll be useless for a while. The doctor says it will take months before I can do much around the farm again. You don't need some random invalid living there. You need someone who—"

"You're right. I don't need some invalid living there, but I do need *you* to be living there. At least you know how to run the place profitably. Your church is helping for now. I can hire more help later, and Brady is planning to stay until you are completely back on your feet, but he could use your experience and guidance."

"If you're sure." He closed his eyes. "My *mamm* and *daett* would take me in, or any of my sisters."

"Of course, they would." I pretended to consider it. "You know, perhaps it would be best if you went to stay with Martha for a few months—just until you are all better. She'd take really good care of you."

I knew he adored his oldest sister but considered her to be the bossiest Amish woman on the planet.

The reality of living with Martha crept over his face. "No!" His eyes popped open. "Please! I'd rather…"

He realized I was teasing.

"You've been around Ellen too long," he said.

The physical therapist came in just then. She was a strong-looking woman who had brought crutches and a therapy belt to put around Lucas's middle to help hold him up in case he fell.

"Ready for your walk, Sweetie?" she asked.

Sweetie?

Lucas said nothing, but I could tell he wasn't happy.

"Can I help?" I asked.

"Yes," Lucas said. "By leaving."

"Excuse me?"

"Leave," he said as the therapist moved the crutches closer to his chair. "Don't watch me try to walk."

"He really is doing well," the therapist chirped as I went out the door. "Just a few problems with balance. Now, just slide off the chair slowly, Honey. Yes! That's a good boy."

58

As I left, I made a mental note to suggest to his family that, if possible, they request a different physical therapist before Lucas realized she was talking to him like a puppy.

CHAPTER 10

"Again," Lucas said through gritted teeth, sweat beading on his forehead as he attempted to button his shirt for the third time. His fingers trembled with effort, but there was steel in his voice.

A man from housekeeping was busy disinfecting various surfaces while Kim, the new physical therapist, watched over Lucas as he struggled.

"You are doing well, Mr. Hershberger," she said. "Most patients don't attempt this level of fine motor work until week six or seven. Your baseline coordination must have been exceptional."

"Farmer," Lucas said simply, finally slipping the button through its hole. "I need to get back to work."

Kim glanced at me, then back at Lucas. "I've seldom seen recovery progress like this from someone with your level of injury. Let's take a brief rest and..."

"Again," Lucas said, reaching for the next button with trembling fingers.

Kim folded her arms, glanced at me, and raised her eyebrows. "Is he always this determined?"

"No," I said, thinking of the days he worked well past dark, wearing a battery-operated headlamp, while finishing various chores when I could tell he was dead on his feet. "Sometimes he's worse."

Lucas, fiercely focused on buttoning his shirt—ignored us. Kim and I watched on in silence.

I decided that maybe this was as good a time as any to ask him about the bridle.

"When I was at your house a couple of weeks ago, I saw something you had been working on."

No response. He was way too busy concentrating on that button.

"It was a bridle you had been polishing."

This time, all I got was a grunt. He wasn't interested in the bridle.

"I finished polishing it for you."

He started on the next button.

"The large medallion had an insignia on it."

He looked at me while still working on that button. I had his attention.

"It was an eagle with a swastika in its claws."

His fingers stopped. "N-Nazi?"

"Looked like it to me," I said. "Did you find it in Rick's antique store?"

He shook his head, looked down at his shirt, and began working on the last button. This time things went slightly smoother.

The housekeeper began bagging up trash.

"Found it at the Harvest Thrift Store. In a box…" he said.

A dietary aide entered the room and readied his lunch tray.

Kim continued to work with him as he tried to lift the plastic coffee cup. "Patience, Lucas. Keep your wrist straight. Let the muscles in your forearm do the work. Remember, your mind is learning how to communicate with your body again."

She spoke with the relentless optimism of someone who'd seen miracles happen through sheer persistence. She was trying to help

Lucas relearn a task that should have been simple but had become complex.

His right hand trembled violently, sending coffee sloshing over the rim. The liquid pooled on the lunch tray.

"I feel like a child," Lucas said, his voice tight with frustration. "Worse than a child. Children can learn."

"You might *feel* like a child. You *are* someone whose brain is building new highways around damaged areas." Kim reached for paper towels. "The pathways that controlled fine motor skills got disrupted. Your brain is literally rewiring itself, creating new connections. It's incredibly sophisticated work, but it takes time."

I watched with sympathy. Every task that had once been automatic for Lucas now required intense concentration and multiple attempts. Buttoning his shirt took twenty minutes and left him exhausted. Writing his name looked like the work of a kindergartner on a sugar rush. Kim had told me that walking ten feet with his crutches had required two rest stops.

The cognitive testing had been encouraging—his memory was largely intact, his speech was improving, his problem-solving abilities seemed unaffected. But his body apparently felt like a constant betrayal to him, refusing to obey commands he felt his mind was sending clearly.

"Let's try something different," Kim suggested, clearing away the lunch tray and reaching for a bag she'd brought. "Work tasks you'd actually do at home."

She laid out a small toolkit—screwdriver, a deliberately loosened furniture joint, and screws of various sizes. Real-world problems instead of therapy exercises.

"Show me how to fix this," she said.

Lucas examined the problem with the methodical attention I remembered from watching him work around the farm. His mind knew exactly what needed to be done—remove the loose screws, apply wood glue to the joint, reassemble with firm pressure. A five-minute job on his worst day.

While he worked with the tools, Kim monitored him while she chatted with me.

"An old bridle with a swastika, huh?"

"Clutched in an eagle's claws."

"Interesting. Did you know that there was so much anti-German war hysteria in this area during World War I that our neighboring town, Berlin, changed the pronunciation of its name? Instead of BerLIN, it's officially pronounced BERlin."

"I knew it was pronounced differently, but I didn't know why."

"My husband is a high-school history teacher. Some of the older folks from this area have told him it was rough around here during World War I and II. Just speaking German was something to avoid."

"I had no idea."

"Even the editor of The Budget got put in jail for just publishing a letter saying Mennonites and Amish shouldn't buy liberty bonds."

While we talked, Lucas was having trouble. When he tried to manipulate the screwdriver, his hands kept betraying him. The tool slipped, skittered across the screw head, and refused to turn with any consistency. After several minutes of struggle, he threw the tools down in disgust.

"My hands don't work right anymore," he said. His jaw was clenched so tightly I wondered if he was damaging his teeth.

"They will," Kim said with the confidence of someone who'd guided hundreds of patients through similar therapy. "Two weeks ago, you could barely hold a spoon. Last week you couldn't button a button. Now you're attempting precision mechanical tasks."

I saw a look of despair cross his face despite her encouraging words, and I longed to comfort him, but my words would mean nothing—I knew no more than he did.

"Your brain is healing faster than most patients I work with," she said carefully. "Will you be exactly the same as before? Maybe, maybe not. But, Mr. Hershberger, I've seen people recover function nobody thought was possible. The difference is often in how hard they're willing to work and how long they're willing to wait for results. And you are obviously a hard worker."

"How long?"

I watched her weigh honesty against hope.

"Months, maybe a year." She handed him the screwdriver again. "The question isn't whether you'll be able to work—it's what kind of work you'll do. Maybe your hands will be steady enough for carpentry again. Maybe they won't. But you'll find ways to work because that's the person you are."

Lucas stared at the tools, then at his hands. "And if I never get better?"

"Then you'll adapt. You'll discover that your value isn't just in what your hands can do."

After the session, she helped Lucas move into a wheelchair, and I took him to a hospital courtyard I'd discovered.

We sat in the shade of a small tree, watching afternoon shadows lengthen across carefully maintained flower beds. Lucas took a few moments to process the day's victories and defeats.

"I want to feel like myself again," he said finally.

"What does that mean?"

"Strong. Able to solve problems instead of *being* one." He held out his disobedient hands. "I can't even hold a coffee cup, Amy."

I thought about my journey since inheriting Rick's farm, about how identity could shift and grow in unexpected directions.

"Do you remember what you told me when I first moved here and couldn't tell a weed from a vegetable?"

A slight smile crossed his features. "That it just takes time and practice."

"And what else?"

"And that there are many ways to be helpful."

"Right. So maybe the question isn't whether you'll be exactly the same helpful as you were before. Maybe it's what new kind of helpful you'll become."

He sat absorbing this.

"I'll accept whatever the Lord sends." He gave me a self-deprecating smile that usually preceded a confession. "But I might not be happy about it for a while."

CHAPTER 11

"Mr. Hershberger," Dr. Peterson said. "What you've accomplished usually takes much longer. Don't let that make you think you're completely healed. The brain needs time to fully recover, even when the body seems ready."

"I understand," Lucas said.

"We're discharging you earlier than typical," Dr. Peterson said, "but with strict conditions. Outpatient physical therapy three times a week, no heavy lifting, no climbing, and if you experience any confusion, severe headaches, or vision changes, you come back immediately."

"We'll watch out for him," I said, including Brady, Lucas's sisters, his parents, and about two hundred church members in my statement.

"I appreciate all you've done." Lucas looked longingly at the door. "But I need to get home, Doctor."

One month after his accident, including seven harrowing days of Lucas fighting to get out of his hospital bed and back on his feet—with or with no one's help—Brady and I brought him home. I think the hospital staff was relieved to see this stubborn man go.

"Easy does it," Brady said, positioning himself on Lucas's right side as we helped him from my car. "We've got all day. No rushing."

The distance from car to door—maybe thirty feet of familiar ground—might as well have been thirty miles. Lucas carefully used his crutches to navigate, each step requiring calculation and effort. Dark circles shadowed his eyes, and I could see him fighting to control his breathing.

Watching this formerly capable man struggle with his own steps drove home exactly how much the accident had stolen from him. His left leg, still in its cast, made it necessary for him to use the crutches as support for his sort of walk, hop, movement. Which made his ribs, still wrapped tightly, hurt. Each step looked like an act of sheer willpower rather than simple locomotion.

Naomi appeared in the doorway wearing a smile that couldn't quite hide her dismay. The son who'd left for town four weeks ago on horseback bore little resemblance to the man struggling up the front steps.

"*Willkumm hoam, mei sei,*" she said, her voice thick with emotion.

"*Danki, Mamm,*" Lucas replied, then translated for Brady and me: "She says welcome home, my son."

The interior of the *Daadi Haus* had been carefully reorganized with his limitations. The comfortable recliner I'd bought online had been delivered. Now it sat near his usual spot by the window—soft enough to support his healing body, sturdy enough to help him stand when his strength gave out.

"I hope you don't mind the changes," I said, suddenly uncertain. "I thought you might be more comfortable..."

"It's perfect." Lucas eased into the chair with a sigh of relief. For a moment, his controlled facade cracked, and I saw how much this simple journey had cost him.

Regina appeared from the kitchen armed with lists and instructions that betrayed her anxiety.

"Everything's labeled," Regina announced, opening cabinets to show her organization system. "Meals in the freezer by date, medications sorted by time of day. Blue container for morning pills, green for evening. Don't skip doses just because you feel a little better one day."

"*Schweschder...*" Lucas's voice carried the patient tone of someone who'd spent thirty-one years being organized within an inch of his life by his loving female relatives.

"And I've stocked enough food for two weeks, brought extra blankets, moved your books within reach..." Her words tumbled out. "The church women will take turns bringing meals, but don't feel obligated to eat if you're not hungry. The doctor said appetite comes back gradually."

"Regina." Lucas's voice was firmer now, gentle but authoritative. "I'll be fine."

She stopped mid-sentence, her hands finally still on the kitchen counter.

"I know you will," she said. "I just... when they called that night, when they said you might not..." She couldn't finish the sentence.

Brady stepped forward with surprising gentleness for such a physically imposing man. "Ma'am, excuse me, but I've been where Lucas is. Busted up, frustrated, feeling like half a man. The hardest part isn't the healing—it's accepting that it takes time. In fact, that'll be the hardest part for the people who love him, too."

Lucas looked up at this unexpected ally, seeing past the cowboy exterior to someone who understood what it meant to have to rebuild from the inside out after being broken.

"How long?" Lucas asked. "Before you felt normal again?"

"Define normal." Brady's smile was rueful. "If you mean exactly like before—never. Capable? About six months. Maybe a year before I stopped being angry about what I'd lost and started appreciating what I'd kept."

"Which was?"

"Life." Brady glanced at me. "The chance to figure out what mattered."

We spent the next hour helping Lucas navigate his transformed space. All tasks that were once routine now demanded strategy. Getting from chair to kitchen required rest stops. Reaching books on top shelves meant accepting help. Even simple things like opening a jar or turning pages had become complex operations.

I watched his frustration build with each small failure, saw the exact moment when his pride collided with his new reality.

"This is humiliating," he said after dropping a water glass for the second time.

"This is temporary," Brady corrected, though we all suspected some changes might be permanent.

"You don't know that."

"That's true," I admitted. "Brady doesn't know if it's temporary, and neither do I. Even the doctors can't tell us. But this is what I know: You are alive. You're going to fight like a wildcat to get better because that's who you are, and you will not have to do it alone."

"Amy..." His voice carried warning and gratitude in equal measure.

"We're not going anywhere, Lucas. None of us. We'll be here to help—just like you would be for any of us."

He nodded slowly, accepting my words. "Thank you."

After his family finally left, Lucas, exhausted by the ordeal of coming home, dozed fitfully in his new chair while I pretended to work on my laptop, marveling that he was here at all.

When he stirred and opened his eyes, the first thing he saw was me.

"You're still here."

"Where else would I be?" I closed my laptop.

"Your real life. New York."

"Lucas, this *is* my real life." I walked over and kneeled beside him.

"Even if I'm never the same?"

"Even if you're never the same."

Lucas thought that over while studying my face in the afternoon light. "You truly mean that."

"Yes, I do."

"That woman," he said finally. "The one in the buggy. Do you know what happened to her?"

"Ida? She's fine. Bruised but fine."

"Good." His eyes drifted closed again.

"Lucas?"

"*Hmm?*"

"I'm so grateful you are alive."

I thought he'd fallen asleep again, but then his hand moved across the armrest of his chair, palm up, an invitation. I slipped my fingers into his, felt them close around mine with strength that was returning day by day.

"Thank you," he said softly. "For staying. For the chair. For not running away."

"Thank you for coming back to us, Lucas." I carefully released his hand even though I wanted to cling to it. "This farm needs you."

CHAPTER 12

Lucas lay in his own bed for the first time in four weeks, listening to the familiar sounds of the *Daadi Haus* settling around him. Every noise was precious—the soft tick of his wall clock, the whisper of wind through the oak tree outside his window, the distant lowing of cattle Brady was managing in the far pasture. Sounds that had once meant home and safety now felt like they belonged to someone else's life.

He'd sent Amy back to the main house two hours ago, insisting he needed to manage on his own. The truth was more complicated. Having her there reminded him of how far he'd fallen from the man he used to be. Every careful movement she made around him, every worried glance, reminded him he was broken.

The crutches leaned against his bed like a monument to his limitations. Dr. Peterson had been clear—at least two more weeks before he could transition into a walking cast, and that was only if his balance improved.

The simple act of getting ready for bed had exhausted him. Buttoning his shirt still took three times longer than normal, and his right hand had developed that tremor again—the one that appeared whenever he pushed too hard. Four weeks ago, he could have worked from dawn to dusk without breaking a sweat. Now, staying awake until eight o'clock felt like an accomplishment. Even climbing into bed was a challenge. Leg casts were heavy.

The man who'd managed this farm with such competence, who could lift hay bales and repair farm equipment, no longer existed. This morning, it had taken him three attempts to pour water from a pitcher into a glass without spilling.

Light spilled through Amy's kitchen window. She was probably making her evening tea, maybe working on one of her writing projects. The routine they'd developed during his last two weeks of recovery—her bringing him books, sitting with him while he struggled through physical therapy exercises, reading to him when his head ached too much to focus—had become precious to him in ways he couldn't afford to examine too closely.

But tonight, lying alone in the darkness, he couldn't avoid the truth any longer. Somewhere between the first day she'd arrived at the farm and this moment, Amy Stanton had become far more than his employer or even his friend. She'd become the person he most wanted to see when he opened his eyes in the morning, the one whose voice could calm him when pain made him restless, the one whose laugh could make him forget, for a few minutes, how broken he felt.

Which was precisely the problem.

Lucas shifted carefully in his bed, wincing as his ribs protested the movement, careful not to twist his bad leg. Four months ago, he'd told Amy that he needed to look for an Amish wife. Someone who shared his faith, who could help him raise children in the traditions he'd been taught to value. Someone… appropriate.

The message was clear. He needed someone who was not her. They had drawn close as they'd searched for his brother-in-law Samuel together. They'd grown even closer when he accompanied her to meet her father for the first time. She'd needed to know the realities before anything more happened between them. Explaining that he would need to find an Amish wife seemed like wisdom and a kindness at the time.

But somehow, even after she left for New York, he hadn't got around to finding anyone, or even looking. He'd told himself that he was too busy, but the truth was—his heart just wasn't in it.

Still, the accident hadn't changed those facts. If anything, it had made them more urgent. His wife had been gone and buried for three years now. He was no longer a young man. Most of his male friends already had a houseful of children. If he were going to build a family, he needed to start soon. And he needed to stop letting himself imagine a future that could never exist.

Amy deserved better than to love a man who came with conditions and limitations. She deserved someone who could offer her the freedom to be herself, not someone who would always be pulled between two worlds. And he deserved a wife who wouldn't have to choose between loving him and living the life she'd built for herself.

The logical thing would be to put distance between them. Stop depending on her for company during his recovery. Stop noticing the way her face lit up when she talked about something that excited her, or the way she unconsciously twisted a strand of hair around her finger when she was deep in thought.

Most of all, he needed to stop allowing himself to fall in love with her more each day.

But lying there in the darkness, Lucas thought about the afternoon she'd driven across three states to sit on the floor of the hospital waiting room, or reading Bible verses aloud to him she didn't really understand because she thought it might help him heal. The fierce protectiveness in her voice when she'd told him she wasn't going anywhere. The way she'd looked at him when he'd finally opened his eyes—like he was something incredibly precious she thought she'd lost forever.

Maybe what he deserved and what he wanted didn't have to be the same thing. Maybe being practical wasn't always the same as being faithful.

The thought felt so dangerous he pushed it away, focusing instead on the immediate challenges. Tomorrow he would start taking longer walks with his crutches so he could build back his stamina. Eventually, he would begin working with Brady on minor jobs on the farm. He would prove to himself and everyone else that he could still be useful.

And he would figure out how to be Amy's friend and neighbor without letting his heart get any more involved than it already was.

Through the window, Amy's kitchen light went out. Lucas imagined her moving through her evening routine—checking the doors, turning off lights, climbing the stairs to the bedroom that had once belonged to Rick. Settling into the house that she was still learning to call home.

Lucas closed his eyes and tried to pray, but the words wouldn't come. How did you ask God for guidance when what you wanted and what you thought you *should* want were pulling in opposite directions?

Outside, a screech owl called from the oak tree, its voice cutting through the peaceful night. In the distance, he could hear Zedekiah making the soft sounds roosters made when they were settling in for sleep. The sounds of a farm at rest.

But Lucas lay awake long into the night, staring at the ceiling and trying to imagine a future that made sense—one where he could be both the man his community expected him to be and the man his heart was telling him he needed to become if he were ever to be truly happy.

It would be a simple decision if he were *Englisch.* Then he could simply choose to be happy. But happiness was an *Englisch* concept which too often held the right of an individual above the good of the community. For an Amish man, a good life meant always prioritizing obedience and responsibility to the good of the family and to the community.

Trying to figure it out made his mind ache with worry and his body cry out with fatigue. Instead, he tried to think of pleasant thoughts—but the only pleasant thoughts he could think of were ones that involved Amy... and that just started the cycle again until, exhausted and in pain, he fell into a restless sleep.

CHAPTER 13

L ucas had been home for two weeks, and he was getting better in small increments most days. The continued physical therapy sessions I took him to tended to wear him out for the entire following day, but so far, so good.

Erma often arrived with a different remedy for him to try—ginkgo tea for his memory, lavender oil for the headaches that still plagued him, and a salve made from herbs she grew herself.

"*Englisch* medicine is good for fixing what's broken," she said. "But Amish medicine is for helping the body remember how to heal itself."

The steady stream of visitors was an eye-opener. Many seemed to energize Lucas in ways the medical treatments and therapy couldn't. His nephew Benjamin's excited chatter about school, Ellen's gentle teasing, even Bishop Noah's quiet presence—each connection seemed to knit another piece of his old self back together.

"Community healing," Brady observed to me one evening. "It's like they're willing him back to himself, one visit at a time."

I kept waiting for single Amish women to come by. I steeled myself to keep my bargain and be welcoming, but except for his sister, Ellen, there didn't seem to be any single women beating a path to his door. It appeared that Amish women married young and stayed married. Because of my promise to God, I tried not to be too thrilled, but it wasn't my fault if no potential Amish wife showed up.

"How come there aren't any single ladies beating a path to your door?" I teased him one day. "I thought you'd be covered up with casseroles and marriage proposals by now from contenders."

"You don't realize how many women I'm related to around here," Lucas said. "It's safer to travel farther outside my community if I'm going to look for a wife."

"Safer?"

"In recent years we have learned that it's wise to have a deeper gene pool when contemplating having children," he said. "Look it up."

I didn't have to look it up to know he was right.

One heartbreaking thing for me, though, was seeing him watch the work on the farm take place around him without being able to fully take part. Brady and the others consulted with him daily, but Lucas was more of a doer than a talker, and it was hard for him to sit on the porch watching the harvesting of his crops being done by others.

He tried to hide it, but by three o'clock each afternoon, his face would go gray with exhaustion. The tremor in his hands got worse when he was tired, and words came slower, as though his brain was working harder to find them.

"I've seen it before," Dr. Peterson said during one of our three-times-a-week visits for checkups and physical therapy. "Your people push through pain better than anyone, but healing isn't about pushing —it's about patience."

"I don't have time to be patient," Lucas told her. "I have too much work to do."

He wasn't wrong. I didn't know how much longer the other Amish community members would be willing to help take care of things.

Now that things had stabilized a bit, I was determined to take care of something I'd let slide too long.

I'd been staring at the letter Rick had left me, reading and rereading his confession and careful instructions about returning the items he had "borrowed" from Sotheby's. Even though I'd found this letter months ago, I hadn't been thinking clearly when I'd escaped to New York in the spring. The last thing on my mind was Rick's issues, and I'd left the letter behind without giving it more than a moment's thought.

In it also were details about my mother's past that I was still trying to process. In fact, they were so far-fetched I wasn't certain they were true. She and I would have to have a serious talk when I saw her again, but I did not know when that would be.

I felt a little guilty about having ignored this letter for so long. After leaving me everything he owned, Rick had only asked this one task from me. I'd been so focused on my own life, I'd let this crucial task slide.

The Nazi bridle sat wrapped in an old towel in Rick's study. It presented another problem I hadn't decided how to handle. Lucas hadn't seemed all that interested in it. I didn't know the bridle's story, but it could probably wait. After all, it belonged to Lucas, and he was already struggling with enough.

Some days it seemed like we had the old Lucas back again. I could almost pretend nothing had happened. On other days he had difficulty with the simplest tasks, slurred his words, and slept most of the day. For now, I thought it would be best to keep things as simple as possible.

Fortunately, Rick had left explicit instructions about what to do with the Sotheby's items. He'd given me a specific person to contact and a path forward. It was time to stop procrastinating.

Zelda Bloom's name was right there in Rick's careful handwriting, along with a note saying she was "trustworthy and discreet." I could only hope that was still true, or that she still worked for the company after all these years.

I remembered her well. As a word-obsessed child, I thought Zelda Bloom had the most wonderful name. I also remember staring at the crystal bowl of Werther's butterscotch candies she kept on her desk. After a while, she gave me free access to the candy bowl every time Rick brought me to work with him.

Finding her contact information on the Sotheby's website didn't take long. Dr. Zelda Bloom, Senior Appraiser, Decorative Arts & Antiquities. Her professional photo showed a woman in her early seventies with silver hair and wide dark eyes that suggested she didn't suffer fools gladly.

I composed the email carefully, attaching a scan of Rick's confession letter and the list of stolen items.

Dr. Bloom,
You may not remember me, but I'm Amy Stanton, Rick Downey's stepdaughter. I have a difficult situation that I hope you can help me resolve privately. Rick passed away last year and left me a letter detailing some items he borrowed from Sotheby's during his career. He gave me instructions to return them, but I need guidance on how to do this without damaging his reputation posthumously. He specifically suggested I contact you.
I've attached his letter and the inventory list. Please let me know if you're able to help. I also have another small issue to discuss with you if you have time.
Sincerely,
Amy Stanton

I'd hesitated over the word "borrowed," but I had loved Rick, and it seemed disloyal after his many kindnesses to use the word "stole." I also wondered if it was presumptuous to ask such an important appraiser to maybe look at the old bridle Lucas had found, but I didn't know who else to ask.

I hit send before I could second-guess myself, then immediately worried that I should have been more formal, more apologetic, more something. But it was done.

My laptop chimed with an almost immediate email notification.

Zelda Bloom responded.

Ms. Stanton,
Of course I remember. You were Rick's adorable little stepdaughter who used
to fill her pockets with my butterscotch.
I am deeply saddened to hear of Rick's passing. I've reviewed his letter and
inventory list. While this situation is certainly delicate, it's not insurmount-
able. I'd prefer to discuss the details by phone rather than email. Are you
available for a call this evening?
Best regards, Zelda

Relief washed over me. She was willing to help, and she didn't sound judgmental about Rick's transgressions. I sent her my phone number and suggested she call in an hour.

In precisely one hour, my phone buzzed and Zelda Bloom's name appeared on the screen. I'd been in the process of pulling my laptop from my tote bag and sat it on top of a stack of books I'd left on the table.

"Hello."

"This is Zelda Bloom speaking."

Her voice was crisp and professional, with a trace of a New York accent. She sounded exactly like someone should sound when they had spent decades evaluating priceless objects and dealing with complicated ownership issues.

"Dr. Bloom, thank you so much for responding so quickly. I wasn't sure if you'd be willing to help."

"Rick was a good friend and a brilliant appraiser who apparently made a few poor life choices—one of which was marrying your mother. I'm happy to help." Papers rustled in the background. "I've printed it out and have been reviewing the list he sent. These are significant pieces. That he kept such detailed records suggests he always intended to return them."

I let the comment about my mother pass. Zelda wasn't wrong.

Desiree had been a very poor choice for Rick. "Can it be done quietly?"

"If we can do this before my retirement, which is due to happen in exactly eight days. My replacement did not know Rick and will not be as… let's say… understanding about this problem. I still have enough influence at Sotheby's to handle this as an administrative correction rather than a theft investigation. Rick's reputation will remain intact, but we must hurry."

The relief was so intense I felt lightheaded. "Thank you. I can't tell you how much this means to me. I'll box them up and send them tomorrow."

"I don't think so." Her disdain was instantaneous. "I will not allow some young man in brown shorts to deliver Rick's stolen treasures to me in a squashed cardboard box. I'll fly out sometime this week to courier them back here where they belong. I'll let you know when to expect me."

This was a surprise. I hadn't thought the items Rick had kept were worth a lot—just an old alarm clock, a small picture by a painter I'd never heard of, and a few small carved animals, which I'd played with as a child. His instructions had directed me to gather the items from a large chest he'd kept locked in his antique store. It was going to be a relief to hand them over.

"While I have you on the phone, I'm curious about something else you mentioned in your email. You said you had another issue to resolve?"

"Yes," I laid the palm of my hand on the towel-covered bridle. "My farm manager found a German horse's bridle with Nazi symbols. I'm not sure what to do with it—or if I should do anything with it."

The silence on the other end of the line stretched long enough that I wondered if we'd been disconnected.

"Dr. Bloom?"

"I'm here." Her voice had changed, becoming sharper and more focused. "Can you describe this bridle?"

I told her about the silver fittings, the medallion with the eagle and swastika that had emerged from beneath decades of tarnish, as well as the name.

"And you found this among Rick's possessions?"

"No. Not Rick's. It was in a box of old horse tack that my farm manager found at a local Amish/Mennonite thrift store. The bridle seems to be of exceptional quality."

"Amy, I need you to listen to me carefully. Assuming this is the real thing and not a duplicate—Nazi artifacts, especially high-quality ceremonial pieces, can attract a very specific type of collector—someone with whom you would not want to get involved. They are not necessarily people who are interested in historical preservation."

"What kind of people are they?"

"The kind who see Nazi symbols as something to celebrate rather than condemn. The kind who will pay enormous sums for authentic pieces, and they aren't buying them for museums." Her voice carried years of expertise, shadowed by personal concern. "If word gets out that you have this bridle, you could attract a lot of unwanted attention."

My mind whirled. "What should I do?"

"I advise you not to post about it online, mention it to anyone else, or contact any dealers." She paused. "Would you be willing to let me examine it when I come to collect the articles Rick wanted returned?"

"That would be so kind of you."

"It isn't kindness. My grandparents died in the Holocaust. Objects like this… they matter to me personally, not just professionally. If this bridle has a story to tell, it should be told properly, not sold to the highest bidder."

CHAPTER 14

The call that complicated everyone's life came on Saturday afternoon. The number on the display was unfamiliar, but I had received a couple of important calls from the hospital with unknown numbers, so I was afraid to let it go to voicemail. I answered, and then immediately wished I hadn't.

"Ms. Stanton?" The voice was male, with the faintest trace of an accent I couldn't place.

"Yes?"

"My name is Klaus Weber. I understand you recently acquired a German military bridle, circa 1940s." He sounded like someone accustomed to getting exactly what he wanted. "I'm prepared to offer you eighteen thousand dollars for it, cash, with immediate pickup."

I almost dropped the phone. My other hand reached for the kitchen counter to steady myself.

"I'm sorry, who is this?"

"A private collector. The piece you have—silver fittings, eagle and swastika medallion—I know exactly what it's worth to the right buyer. This is a very generous offer, Ms. Stanton."

"How do you know what I have?"

"Word gets around in certain circles. Items like this… they have a way of surfacing. My clients pay well for authentic pieces."

My mouth went dry. The only people I could think of who knew about it were Lucas, Zelda, and me. Maybe Brady. I couldn't remember whether I'd said anything to him about it yet.

"What circles?" I managed.

"Discerning collectors of historical artifacts. People who appreciate the significance of such pieces." There was a pause, and when he spoke again, his tone had sharpened slightly. "Twenty thousand will be my last offer. But I need an answer today."

"I'm not interested in selling."

"Ms. Stanton, I don't think you understand the situation. It would be much better for everyone, including your friend, Mr. Hershberger, if this piece found its way to a private collection where it can be properly appreciated."

He knew about Lucas? Was this a threat? I felt cold despite the warm afternoon sunshine streaming through the kitchen window.

"I said I'm not interested."

"I'll call back tomorrow. In the meantime, think carefully about my offer."

The line went dead.

I stood frozen in the kitchen, phone still pressed to my ear, trying to process what had just happened. Twenty thousand dollars. For an old horse's bridle in a cardboard box at a local thrift store.

I marched over to the *Daadi Haus* and knocked. Soon, I heard the thump of his crutches. My face must have shown that I was upset when he opened the door. This was bad. Really bad. I wished Zelda were here, but she wasn't due to come until tomorrow.

"Amy," he said. "What's wrong?"

I walked into his living area on unsteady legs. "Someone just offered us twenty thousand dollars for your Nazi bridle. That's what's wrong."

Lucas fell into his seat by the window. He looked as befuddled as I felt. "Who? And why?"

"A man named Klaus Weber. He knew specific details about it—the silver fittings, the eagle medallion." My voice was shaking now. "Lucas, how could he possibly know about it?"

"Did he say how he found out?"

"Just that 'word gets around in his circles.' Whatever that means." I sank into the chair across from him. "And when I refused to sell, he made it sound like… like keeping it might not be safe. He mentioned you by name."

Lucas's face was grave. "The bridle must be worth a lot more than we realized."

"But how did he find out about it? I've been so careful. The only people who know are you, me, and Zelda. And maybe Brady, but I don't think so."

"Sounds like Zelda must have mentioned it to the wrong person."

I grabbed my phone and texted Zelda Bloom.

"A stranger just offered me $20,000 for the bridle. I don't know how they found out about it. Did you say something to someone, because we didn't."

I hit send.

My phone rang again. Same unknown number as before.

I didn't answer. Then the voicemail notification chimed. I played it on speaker.

"Ms. Stanton, this is Klaus Weber again. I wanted to clarify something —I'm not the only person interested in your acquisition. There are others who may not be as reasonable in their approach. I'm offering you a clean transaction, no questions asked. I strongly suggest you consider it."

The message ended.

Lucas and I stared at each other across the small living room. Outside, I could hear Brady working with the cattle, the sounds of a peaceful farm afternoon. Inside, everything felt like it had shifted into something darker and more dangerous.

"What do you think we should do?" I asked.

"It doesn't sound like Klaus wants to put it in a museum," Lucas said. "What do you think Rick would do if he were here?"

It was a good question, and it helped clarify my thoughts. "I doubt he would have allowed it to disappear into a private collection where it would be lost, or even worse—idolized."

My phone buzzed with a text. Zelda Bloom had already responded.

"I have said nothing to anyone. Your message concerns me greatly. I'll be in Ohio tomorrow. This is not something you should handle alone."

Relief flooded through me so suddenly I felt dizzy. Help was coming—someone with expertise and experience. Someone Rick had trusted.

"Zelda will be here tomorrow," I told Lucas. "She says this isn't something to handle alone."

"Good. The sooner, the better." He moved his bad leg and winced. "Until she arrives, answer no more calls from unknown numbers."

"Of course not."

My phone buzzed again. A text from the same unknown number:

"Time is a factor, Ms. Stanton. Don't wait too long to decide."

I showed the text to Lucas, who watched me with a stalwart expression, despite the pain that still marked his features.

"Whatever happens," he said, "I would feel better if you hid the bridle and locked your doors tonight."

I nodded in agreement. "I'll also ask Brady to sleep in the guest bedroom instead of his RV."

"That's wise."

As the afternoon shadows lengthened across the farm, I couldn't shake the feeling that we'd crossed some invisible line into territory neither of us understood. And somewhere out there, people we'd never met were apparently making plans that involved an artifact hidden in my house—plans that probably didn't include our safety.

Zelda couldn't come soon enough.

CHAPTER 15

Zelda arrived like an academic warrior armed with what appeared to be half the reference section of the New York Public Library.

I watched from the kitchen window as she emerged from a rented gray sedan, wrestling an enormous satchel from the passenger seat. The bag looked like it weighed more than she did, but she handled it with the practiced efficiency of someone who'd been hauling research materials around for decades.

"She's here," I called to Brady, who had been getting dressed. My father had spent the night, and we'd stayed up late exchanging stories we had never gotten to talk about. I still didn't know how long he would stay to help me, but I already dreaded his leaving. I loved having my father around, even when he wasn't repairing leaking plumbing.

"The antique expert from New York?" Brady was immediately at my side.

"That would be her." I opened the front door before she could knock, partly out of politeness and partly because I was genuinely excited about getting to see her again after all these years.

Zelda Bloom was exactly as I remembered her from my childhood. The only change was the color of her hair, and there might have been a few wrinkles that weren't there when I'd known her. She stood maybe five-foot-three in sensible black shoes, wearing a navy cardigan that had seen better decades and carrying herself with the no-nonsense authority of someone accustomed to being the smartest person in the room. Her silver hair was pulled back in a practical bun held in place with what looked like a vintage hairpin, and she wore reading glasses on a beaded chain that caught the afternoon light.

"Amy? It is so wonderful to see you again, although I wish it were under different circumstances." Her handshake was firm, her voice cultured and efficient with the expertise of someone who'd spent years cutting through Manhattan small talk. "Thank you for calling about Rick's situation. And I'm very sorry for your loss."

"Thank you so much for coming all this way." I was so thrilled to see her, I practically curtsied.

"Nonsense. It's no trouble. I need to take care of this before I retire. I fear that my replacement, who never knew Rick, will feel the need to make this public." She hefted her satchel with both hands. "Besides, when you mentioned the German military bridle, I knew I had to see it myself."

I led her into the living room. Brady had helped bring Lucas over so he could be part of the conversation. I could tell that Lucas was attempting to appear more alert than he felt. He'd worked especially hard this week. His walking with crutches was steadier, and his speech had lost most of the careful deliberation that had marked his first weeks home—but afternoons still hit him hard.

"Zelda, this is my father, Brady Maddox, and Lucas Hershberger. He manages the farm."

"You are the one who found the bridle." Zelda studied him with frank curiosity, the way she might examine an interesting piece of pottery. "How are you feeling?"

"Better each day, thank you." Lucas's natural reserve seemed to intensify under her direct gaze.

"Good." She heaved her satchel on the coffee table with a thump that made the lampshade quiver. "Now then, shall we start with Rick's little problem, or would you prefer to show me this mysterious German artifact first?"

I glanced at Lucas, who nodded slightly. "Rick's items first, I think."

"Sensible." Zelda opened her satchel and began extracting items with the systematic precision of a surgeon laying out instruments. White cotton gloves, a jeweler's loupe, a magnifying glass with an ornate silver handle, several small tools I couldn't identify, and a notebook that looked like it predated the Kennedy administration.

"You came prepared," Lucas observed as he watched the equipment appear.

"Forty-three years in this business teach you to bring everything you might need." Zelda pulled on the white gloves with practiced movements. "You never know what you'll find, and there's nothing worse than discovering something that might be important and not having the right tools to examine it properly."

I had already retrieved the items Rick had listed from their hiding places around the antique store.

"Ah." Zelda's voice carried a note of recognition and pleasure as she approached the table. "The Fabergé animals."

She picked up the tiny elephant that had been my favorite during childhood visits to Rick's office, turning it carefully in her gloved hands. The miniature creature seemed to glow under the dining room light, every detail perfect despite being no larger than my thumb.

"Genuine, of course. Early 1900s, probably a gift set." She reached for the magnifying glass—the one with the silver handle. "Rick always had exquisite taste, even in his... unauthorized acquisitions."

"You called that magnifying glass Sherlock," I blurted, remembering her tendency to name her tools.

Zelda looked up, startled, then smiled. "Yes, I've had Sherlock for thirty years. He's seen more forgeries than a treasury agent."

She returned to her examination of several adorable and exquisitely made tiny animals carved from semi-precious stone. I especially liked the mischievous-looking squirrel, and the fat little mama pig whose head screwed off, revealing three tiny piglets. Altogether, there were about a dozen various farm animals along with the squirrel and elephant. I had so many memories of playing with them as a child—I wished I could afford to keep them.

"This collection... it's worth considerably more now than when Rick borrowed it. The mother pig is especially valuable. Faberge was known for making secret compartments in some of their works— with hidden treasure within."

I couldn't help but ask, "How much is it all worth?"

"Conservatively? Two hundred thousand, maybe. Who knows? Possibly twice that at auction. If someone wants them badly enough." She set the elephant down with careful reverence. "Your stepfather wasn't just taking pretty baubles, my dear. He was stealing museum-quality pieces."

"Will there be... legal consequences? For me, I mean?"

"None whatsoever. You were a child when these items were taken, and Rick's letter provides clear documentation of his guilt and your innocence." Zelda moved to the Tiffany clock, her expression softening slightly. "Ah—hello there, old friend!"

It took me a moment to realize she was talking to the clock.

"1889. A Tiffany carriage clock. It had an alarm, which was very advanced, and portable to boot. A rarity. There were only 91 of these made." She inspected it. "Hmm. Slightly worn. Worth about ten thousand as is. But at auction? Again—who knows? Sometimes people lose all common sense during an auction—which is something we in the auction business adore."

"But back to legal consequences: Sotheby's would much rather have these pieces returned without fanfare than deal with the publicity of prosecuting a dead man's stepdaughter."

"Just like that?"

"Just like that."

"I'm so grateful I could hug you!"

"Oh, dear." Zelda didn't look up from examining a marking on the clock. "Please don't."

Yes, this was the Zelda I remembered from my childhood.

"The clock sat on my bureau during the years Rick lived with us. The ticking helped me sleep. I did not know it was stolen."

"Of course you didn't." She began carefully wrapping each item in tissue paper she drew from her satchel. "I'll transport these back to New York personally, and they'll be returned to inventory without fuss. As far as anyone will know, they were misplaced because of a clerical error."

The relief I felt was intense. One crisis was resolved, at least. But as Zelda finished packing away my childhood memories, my cell phone rang again.

Klaus—keeping his word about calling back "tomorrow." I didn't answer. In a few seconds, his voice came through, leaving a message, and I put it on speaker.

"I am afraid you did not understand me, Ms. Stanton. Trust me on this. You are not capable of fully appreciating the artifact that has fallen into your possession. I have offered you a fair price. I will be back in touch. You should think hard before you turn my offer down. There are others who, if they hear of it, will not ask so nicely."

He disconnected. His veiled threats were like something from a bad movie. I had no idea even how to feel about it. Should I shrug it off or be terrified?

Zelda, however, knew exactly what to do.

"Now," she said, pulling off her gloves and flexing her fingers, "show me that German bridle."

CHAPTER 16

I led her to Rick's study, where I'd been keeping it. Even wrapped in an old towel, the thing seemed to radiate menace.

Zelda's reaction when I unwrapped it stopped my breath.

Her face immediately went ash-white.

For a long moment, she simply stared, her hands clenched at her sides. I watched decades of professional composure crumble as something intensely personal collided with her expertise.

"Zelda?" I asked. "Are you all right?"

She blinked hard, pulling herself back from wherever the sight of Nazi symbols had taken her. "Forgive me. It never gets any easier. Even after all these years."

But as she pulled on her gloves to examine it, her hands were shaking.

She lifted the bridle with the respect due to something either precious or poisonous, turning it slowly in the light. Through her magnifying glass, she examined every stitch, every piece of metalwork, every detail that could reveal its secrets.

"The leatherwork is Vienna quality," she murmured, more to

herself than to me. "See this stitching pattern? It's distinctive—used exclusively at the Spanish Riding School."

Her voice grew stronger as professional training overtook emotional reaction. "The silver fittings..., the craftsmanship is extraordinary. This wasn't standard military equipment, Amy. This was ceremonial. Custom-made."

"Who do you think it was for?"

"Someone with significant authority. Someone who could afford the finest artisans in Vienna." She set the bridle down carefully, as if it might explode. "Someone who wanted the world to know exactly what he represented."

I pointed to the words "Stute Sokora" stamped into the leather. "Do you know what that means?"

She typed something into her phone. "Ah, here it is. 'Stute' means 'mare'. 'Sokora' is probably the horse's name. Not one I've ever heard, though. Putting a horse's name on their tack is done for the better horses. Apparently Sokora had some worth."

"Fascinating," I said. "I have so many questions."

"And I have connections that can help you find answers, but Amy, listen to me carefully. Klaus Weber isn't just any collector. I made inquiries after our last conversation. He's part of a network that specifically targets Nazi artifacts."

She pulled out her phone again, scrolling rapidly through messages. "I've been getting texts all morning. Word is spreading in certain circles that an SS ceremonial bridle has surfaced in Ohio."

"How could they possibly know?"

"Because someone has been talking to the wrong people." Zelda's voice carried four decades of professional knowledge shadowed by personal anger. "Amy, the Austrian Cultural Ministry contacted me an hour ago. They want this bridle back in Europe for investigation."

"Investigation of what?" I asked.

"To determine if it belonged to one of the officers who escaped to

America after the war." Her hands were steady now, anger burning away fear. "If it did, there could be implications for families, for communities, for people who did not know they were harboring evidence of war crimes."

"What do we do?" I asked.

"First, we get this thing out of your house before Klaus Weber stops asking politely."

For the next half-hour I received an education that I never wanted to have.

Zelda explained that there had been multiple thefts of Nazi memorabilia from Holocaust museums worldwide, as well as break-ins targeting private collectors of WWII memorabilia. Zelda wasn't just being dramatic. That information about the bridle had leaked out truly had put us in danger.

"How about I drive it to Cincinnati?" Brady offered. "There's a Holocaust museum there. I could take it, drop it off, and be back within the day." He brushed his hands together as though ridding himself of the presence of the bridle. "I don't want my daughter to have anything more to do with it."

"Unfortunately, it doesn't work that way," Zelda replied. "There are laws about obtaining Nazi-related items, which sometimes creates a high black market for them. The museum could contact the local FBI, who could choose to investigate. You might all be questioned."

Brady looked a little sick. No one with a prison record wanted the FBI on their doorstep—even if he was presently a rodeo hero.

"It could have been the housekeeper," Lucas said abruptly.

"What do you mean?" I wondered whether this random utterance had anything to do with his brain injury.

"At the hospital," Lucas continued. "When Amy asked me about where I'd gotten the bridle, a housekeeper was cleaning and taking out the trash. We were so used to people coming and going, we didn't even notice. I'm sure he overheard us talking about it."

I felt like kicking myself. Since the man was basically "just" a janitor, he'd been invisible to me. I knew better, but I'd been so focused on talking with Lucas, I hadn't paid attention.

"Or it could have been your physical therapist that day," I remembered. "She said her husband was a history teacher. And then, there was the dietary aide, too."

"That isn't important," Zelda said. "Obviously, the two of you were feeling quite chatty that day. The important thing is that Klaus and his cronies already know."

"Can we just give it to you?" I traced the leather straps with my finger. Everything about it saddened me. "You would know what to do with it. We don't."

"European nations deal with hundreds of Nazi-era artifacts annually. Sometimes there's a matter of restitution—a valuable family heirloom or work of art that needs to be returned. Since the Nazi officer who owned this wasn't a victim, the country's cultural ministry would be the ones to choose the final disposition. It would go either to a museum, secure storage, or be destroyed just to keep it out of the hands of Nazi sympathizers and collectors."

Zelda began wrapping the bridle in the same protective archival wrapping paper she'd brought with her. "I'll take it back to New York with me tonight. Sotheby's has secure storage, and if, as I suspect, it's Austrian, their authorities can take custody from there."

"Is it safe for you to travel with it?"

"Safer than leaving it here with you." She lifted her satchel, ready to go. "Amy, promise me—if Klaus Weber shows up, don't answer the door. Just call the police."

For a split second, I almost wished I were back in New York City. The NYPD would know exactly what to do with someone like Klaus. I didn't know if our village cops here in Sugarcreek would be trained well enough to know how to deal with him.

I've never been more grateful to get rid of something than when

Zelda had me sign a receipt, shoved the bridle in her carry-on luggage, and drove away to the airport.

After she left, I stood in my living room feeling like the walls were closing in. The bridle was gone, but the danger it might represent was not.

CHAPTER 17

L ucas sat in his recliner, thinking about the unfamiliar car he'd
       seen driving slowly past their driveway many times. There was
nothing remarkable about the car and the lone male driver. They were
used to tourists driving on their back roads. Some drove around
simply hoping to spot a sign in an Amish yard advertising something
homemade for sale that they wanted. He didn't blame them. There
was really no telling what they might find being sold out of Amish
back porches. Birdhouses, fry pies, baskets, quilts, fresh eggs, baked
goods, honey, maple syrup.

Still, seeing the same car driving by numerous times over several
days left him with a troubling feeling.

Lucas remembered his grandfather telling him how their community had faced suspicion during both world wars. Their German
heritage, their continued use of the German language, and their
refusal to fight, had made them targets of mistrust and sometimes
outright hostility.

If word got out that Nazi memorabilia had been found here, it
would confirm some ugly suspicions that some people had harbored
about the Amish's loyalties in years past.

Even without a war going on, nearly every Amish person he knew had been subjected to some sort of harassment. Firecrackers being thrown out of passing cars at their horse's feet, purposely making them rear in fright. Mockery of their clothing and lifestyle. Rocks were sometimes thrown at buggies for no other reason than to startle the people inside. There had been loud disruptions of their religious services, and then there was vandalism. For reasons Lucas could not comprehend, crude images of human body parts were sometimes sprayed on their barns and outbuildings. Some *Englisch* had a strange sense of humor.

He hated the fact that he had been the one to bring this trouble to Amy's door—as though he hadn't already caused her enough grief. None of it was intentional, but it still bothered him. He'd been trying to think of some way of thanking her, doing something helpful, at the very least creating something she would consider beautiful.

Carpentry was out. He couldn't stand up long enough. Most of his skills took the kind of physical ability he had not yet regained. Fortunately, his hands had been working better recently. Maybe there was something he could do...

He made his way to the cedar chest at the foot of his bed. Inside, wrapped in an old quilt his grandmother had made, lay the leatherworking tools that had belonged to his grandfather—tools Lucas hadn't touched since the old man's death when Lucas was sixteen.

He unwrapped the quilt and took stock of the tools. The familiar weight of the head knife felt right in his palm despite the years. His grandfather had been a master leatherworker, one of the finest in Holmes County, and he'd insisted that Lucas learn properly.

"A man should know how to work with his hands," the old man had always said. "Leather is honest—it shows every mistake, but it rewards patience and skill."

Lucas had been good at it as a boy, his young fingers nimble with the precise cuts and delicate tooling work. But after his grandfather's death, then marriage and farm responsibilities, the tools had stayed wrapped away. Now, as he examined the familiar stamps and swivel knives, muscle memory stirred.

He'd been watching Amy struggle with that oversized tote bag of hers for too long. She used it as both purse and laptop carrier, and it clearly frustrated her—everything tangled together, nothing in its proper place. A woman who could organize complex research projects and write with such clarity deserved better than digging through chaos every time she needed a pen. He didn't understand why she didn't find something better to carry her things in.

He'd noticed that she was someone who took care of everyone else around her before she thought of herself, and he'd been taking up too much of her time. She'd probably been more organized back in her apartment in New York City, he doubted that she'd gotten settled at all since she'd rushed back to Sugarcreek after his accident.

Lucas enjoyed fixing things and solving problems. The answer to her disorganization was something he had the skill to fix. And since it was something he could do sitting down, he could accomplish it without her or Brady's help.

He decided to create the perfect portable office for her, made of the best leather he could find. Sure, there were other tote bags with pockets Amy could use, but Lucas knew precisely what Amy carried in her bag. He could picture it clearly: a seamless blend of briefcase and tote bag, perfectly sized for her laptop, with compartments for everything she carried. A bag with one main compartment, and two large zipper pockets on each side. Strong straps so that she never had to worry about one breaking. A snap pocket for the charging cord so it wouldn't get tangled, places to keep her pens and pencils in one place and easy to grab. He'd make a pocket for her cell phone, and slots for her business cards. Perhaps she could use one of the zipper pockets to store the two notebooks she always had with her. He would make her a compartment with room for a few little things like lip balm and a small container of aspirin because sometimes Amy got headaches. A latch for her keys. A place to tuck a small package of tissues. Rich brown leather, maybe with some subtle tooling. And on the inside panels…

His mind moved to the scenes he'd been saving in the back of his mind, moments from their relationship that deserved preservation. He would have to ask someone in his family to pick up a nice piece of leather from Weaver's, the kind of leather that would age beautifully, become more supple and rich with years of handling. But until that happened, he could practice honing his skills on the scraps he currently had in his possession.

He selected a piece of scrap leather from the pile and picked up a modeling tool. His hands remembered the motions—the precise pressure needed to create clean lines, the way leather responded to patient, steady work.

An image came to him whole: the view from his *Daadi Haus* overlooking the farm and Amy's front door. He could hide small likenesses of items that had brought the two of them together within the image. A mosaic of their story. He could capture that in leather, using the old techniques his grandfather had taught him for creating dimensional scenes.

Lucas began working slowly, his hands relearning skills he was afraid he had lost. When he set the tools aside hours later, a small section of leather bore the clear outline of a bucket of daffodils sitting on a porch, recognizably Amy's.

Simply saying thank you for all she'd done seemed so shallow compared to the depth of his gratitude to her. This would take weeks, possibly months, to complete according to his vision. Lucas decided he would take all the time in the world to create something truly worthy of the woman who had brought light and laughter back into his life.

Through his window, he could see her pacing on her front porch, phone pressed to her ear. The reception was better out there. She was probably talking to Zelda. Amy's face was animated, her free hand gesturing as she talked, the way it always did when she was working through a problem.

When he first heard Klaus Weber's offer, he'd been secretly tempted. Twenty thousand dollars was a lot of money to a man with hospital debts and nothing in the way of income right now. The bridle meant nothing to him. But he agreed that he and Amy needed to refuse for one reason only—he didn't want anyone of that caliber anywhere near her—not to bring the money, not to pick up the bridle, not even to look at her face.

Bishop Elmer had always preached about the dangers of entanglement with the *Englisch* world. About how their values and ways of life could seduce faithful people away from the narrow path of righteousness. Lucas had listened to those sermons for years, accepting them as wisdom born of experience and scriptural understanding.

But what he saw when he looked at Amy wasn't a threat to his faith, but a woman whose actions consistently showed the kind of love that his faith was supposed to cultivate.

It wouldn't be easy, but he looked forward to seeing the look on her face when he gave her this gift.

CHAPTER 18

L ucas was having a rough day. He'd sat on the porch all morning, watching other people bringing in the hay from his front pasture. He had helped many of them in the past, true, but it was still hard to sit there and watch. He did what he could. Ordered supplies, kept the books, paid the bills, but as he watched Brady work with the cattle in the far pasture, Lucas felt increasingly useless.

Tomorrow it would be eight weeks since his accident, and he felt like he was being forced to sit and watch life happen around him instead of participating in it. He knew that at thirty-two he was in the prime of his life, but if this was what it felt like to be at his peak—he surely hoped it wasn't going to be downhill from here.

He was so nervous he felt like he wanted to crawl right out of his skin. It felt suffocating being trapped like this within his own limitations, being reduced to sitting and watching while other people shouldered his responsibilities in addition to their own. And Lucas? Lucas had been working with leather. Tooling designs like his grandfather had taught him as a boy, before he turned sixteen and decided to focus solely on farm work.

He set aside the leather piece he'd been working on—the front zipper pocket with Amy's initials carefully tooled into the corner—and made his way to the window.

He could see Brady riding Midnight while he checked on the cattle. Lucas liked Brady's way with the horses, but he couldn't help but imagine himself once again being able to swing into the saddle, feeling the horse's power beneath him as they cantered down the road toward town. He remembered the feeling of freedom and the simple joy of riding somewhere just because he wanted to.

But his left leg was still too stiff, his balance too uncertain. Even harnessing a horse to his buggy required a stability he didn't yet possess.

Lucas reached for the three-pronged cane that had become his constant companion. Eight weeks out from the accident, the cast was off, and he had a walking boot. Heavy, but he was a little more mobile now. With the cane and the walking boot, he'd made it to the mailbox and back yesterday.

He wondered if he could walk the mile to town if he went very slow.

Dr. Peterson had been pleased with his progress at last week's appointment. "That farm work really did build exceptional core strength. Your balance is excellent."

Amy's antique store sat empty in town, just one mile away. To his knowledge, no one had checked on it since his accident. Before then, he went at least once a week to make certain there were no leaks or damage. Maybe it was time to test his limits and go look in on it. If he could make it there, he would have a comfortable place to rest before coming home.

He knew he had no business attempting such a walk, but the need to accomplish something, anything, overrode his common sense.

Gathering his keys and a bottle of water, he started down the road at a careful but determined pace.

The first quarter-mile felt manageable. His cane found steady purchase on the gravel, and his leg seemed to cooperate. But by the halfway point, Lucas felt weaker, his leg ached, and he was breathing harder than he'd expected. A fine sheen of sweat beaded his forehead despite the cooler September air.

By the time he reached the store's front door, he was shaking from head to toe with the effort of maintaining his balance. He fumbled with the keys, finally getting the door open and stumbling inside to collapse on the first chair he saw.

Fool. The word echoed in his mind as he tried to catch his breath. He'd exhausted himself walking one mile. Now, his leg was aching, and he was trapped in town with no way to get home except to call for help. The humiliation burned worse than the physical pain.

All of this just because he couldn't bear to spend another day feeling like an invalid.

Now that he was here, he couldn't even do what he'd hoped to accomplish. He'd intended to check all the floors, make certain nothing was leaking, or broken. That's all. Had there been a problem, he would have called someone else to fix it. Now, he couldn't even do that. It was going to be everything he could do just to limp over to the counter, retrieve the keys to Rick's office hanging beneath, so that he could access the store's phone and call Brady.

That was when he heard it—a soft whimpering sound from just outside the front door.

At first, he thought it might be his own unconscious expression of frustration, but then it came again. It sounded like an animal in distress.

Using his cane to lever himself upright, Lucas made his way carefully to the door and peered outside. He saw nothing until a movement near the building's foundation caught his eye.

A dog lay curled against the brick wall, clearly injured and in pain. German Shepherd mix, probably male, with intelligent eyes. But the animal was painfully thin, its coat matted and dull.

"*Ach*, little fellow," Lucas said softly, stepping outside despite his own physical discomfort. "What happened to you?"

The dog's tail gave a weak wag at the gentle tone, and Lucas saw that the dog had clearly been surviving on its own for a long time, growing weaker every day.

Lucas looked at the fatigued animal and saw himself—exhausted, struggling, trying to survive on diminished capabilities. Without hesitation, he made his way back inside and found one of Rick's ceramic bowls. He did not know if it was valuable, and he didn't care. The dog needed water more than the bowl needed preserving.

He filled it from the sink in the bathroom and carried it outside, settling it carefully on the ground beside the animal that was eyeing him with suspicion. The dog seemed to realize that Lucas meant no harm and drank gratefully, its tail wagging stronger now, while Lucas talked to it.

"You're in rough shape, aren't you? But you're a fighter. I can see that in your eyes."

The dog finished drinking and looked up at Lucas with an expression filled with gratitude and trust. In that moment, Lucas made a decision that surprised him with its certainty. It was high time he owned a dog, assuming no one came forward to claim this one.

He went inside the store and used Rick's landline to call Dr. Peggy Oglesby's veterinary clinic, which was just up the street. He was pleased when she was the one who answered. Perhaps her staff had already gone home. It was almost closing time.

"Dr. Oglesby? Lucas Hershberger. I've got a stray dog here at the antique store, and I need help. I—I can't walk reliably yet."

Dr. Oglesby had served as a military veterinarian before settling in Sugarcreek, and she understood both animal trauma and the pride that made some men reluctant to ask for help.

"What kind of dog are we looking at? Are there any injuries?" she asked.

Lucas described what he could see, and Peggy agreed to come as soon as she could close up.

She arrived twenty minutes later. Carl, her veterinarian assistant and husband, was with her. She took one look at the situation and understood immediately that she had not one but two patients who needed care.

"He's dehydrated and malnourished," she said after examining the dog. "But there seems to be no physical injuries, which is good. Also, he doesn't appear to have a microchip to link him to any owner."

"I am sure Amy will be fine with my taking care of him out at the farm while we search for his owner. What will it take to get him healthy again?"

"Time, proper nutrition, and someone who cares enough to see him through the recovery." She glanced at Lucas. "Sound familiar?"

"It does."

While Peggy and Carl coaxed the dog into a travel crate, Carl helped Lucas limp to their car.

"No point in your walking back home when we're heading that direction anyway," he said.

Dr. Peggy sat in the back seat with the dog, while Carl drove them to Lucas's home.

"I'd like to keep him, he told Doctor Peggy as they carefully carried the dog into his house. "If we don't find his owners."

"Might be good for both of you." She smiled. His decision to keep the dog pleased her. "I'll ask around, but with no collar and in this shape—I think you've found yourself a dog."

Carl stroked the dog's fur and talked to it in a low voice. It closed its eyes as though savoring his touch.

"I've never known anyone more in tune with an animal, than my husband." Dr. Peggy looked on fondly. "I'll send him around tomorrow with the necessary shots. We'll get some blood work, too."

"I appreciate all you've done," Lucas said.

"This is what I went to school for," Dr. Peggy said. "Rescuing good dogs is my favorite thing."

"Only good dogs?" Lucas asked.

"They're *all* good dogs," Carl said.

Once Carl and Peggy had gotten Lucas and the dog situated and waved their goodbyes, evening hushed the farm. Lucas lowered himself onto his kitchen floor beside the injured dog, moving carefully.

"What should I call you?" he mused, stroking the dog's head. The animal's eyes were alert, watching Lucas with rapt attention.

The dog's tail thumped against the floor, and Lucas felt something he hadn't experienced since his accident—the sense that maybe God had a purpose for broken things after all, and that maybe walking to town today hadn't been just his foolish pride but necessary obedience to something larger than his own understanding.

Outside, he could hear Brady's truck returning from whatever errand he and Amy had gone on. Amy knocked on the door of the Daadi Haus.

"Come in," Lucas called, "But, be prepared. We have a new visitor."

Amy opened the door, her face slightly concerned at the mention of a visitor, but her eyes lit up when she realized the visitor was the sweet dog lying on the floor.

"Visitor?" she said, dropping to her knees in front of the stray. "No. I think we have a new member of the family!"

"Well, that may be true, but this is one member of the family in need of a bath," Brady said. "Can I use your shower, Lucas?"

When Brady emerged from the bathroom twenty minutes later, he looked like he had been in a rainstorm, but an entirely different dog trotted along beside him. Not only was it clean, it acted like the bath and the attention had given it heart. Brady tossed a clean towel to Amy. "You can finish drying him off. I need to go get me some different clothes. Pretty sure that animal has never been bathed before."

"Thanks, Brady," Lucas said. "I appreciate it."

Brady lifted his hand in acknowledgement as he went out the door.

Amy was sitting on the floor giving the dog a rub down when she said, "What are we going to name him?"

Lucas mentally flipped through a list of dog names he'd heard. He didn't like any of them. Most of them were cutesy, which didn't fit this German Shepherd at all. Despite everything it had been through, there was a special look to this dog. He believed once it had been nursed back to health, he would have a loyal and intelligent companion.

A name came to him he thought might fit.

"Lazarus," he said. "A man who rose from the dead. I think that describes both of us, don't you?"

Amy scrunched up her nose and shook her head.

"What's wrong with the name Lazarus?"

"This dog is way too sweet for such a serious name."

"German Shepard's are a serious breed."

Lucas watched Amy with curiosity. He had forgotten that writers always have strong opinions about naming things.

"I always wanted a dog when I was little. It was never practical, so we never got one, but I had a babysitter who had a German Shepherd named Rusty. I loved that dog. It about killed me when we moved and I never got to see him again. Would you care terribly if we gave this one the same name? Amy looked up at where Lucas was sitting in his chair, her eyes full of hope.

Lucas realized in that moment that he would have let Amy name the dog anything she wanted just to keep her looking at him like that. "Rusty it is, then. A perfect name for a good dog."

Amy looked triumphantly at the dog. "Do you like your new name, Rusty?"

Rusty thumped his tail in response and then rolled over onto his back so that Amy could scratch his stomach. After giving him a good scratch, and a kiss on his snout, she wiped down Lucas's bathroom, gathered up all the wet towels to launder, and said her goodbyes.

After she left, Rusty walked over to the closed front door, put his nose against it and whined softly, as though he already missed her.

"I know how you feel, buddy," Lucas said. "I feel the same way when she leaves."

Life returned to Lucas's usual evening rhythm, but tonight was different. Tonight, he had a companion who understood what it meant to be broken. Together they would heal. Together, maybe they could both figure out how to be useful again.

CHAPTER 19

Lucas tried to find a position that did not send shooting pains through his left leg. The walk to town had done no real damage, but it had not done him any good either. He had a feeling he would be wearing his walking boot and using a cane for a while longer because of it.

Rusty lay at his feet, the dog's breathing deep and even but not fully asleep. In the three days since, Dr. Oglesby had evaluated him, and Carl had given him his shots. Rusty was significantly better in health now that he had access to consistently good food and water. In Lucas's opinion, the German Shepherd's companionship was more helpful than any medicine.

Amy had already fallen head-over-heels in love with Rusty, and Brady wasn't far behind, already trying to teach the dog how to herd cattle. It wasn't going well.

"I don't think he was bred for that," Lucas pointed out.

"It was worth a try," Brady had said. "Next time you get a stray, see if you can't find us a nice, hard-working Border Collie."

"Can't sleep either, can you, boy?" Lucas said softly, reaching down to stroke the dog's head. Rusty's tail thumped once against the floor, and Lucas marveled at how much comfort this animal was providing.

Then suddenly, the dog's ears pricked forward, with every muscle in his body going on alert. A low rumble started in his throat—not yet a growl, but close.

"What is it?" Lucas whispered, straining to hear whatever had caught the dog's attention.

Then he heard it—the nearly silent hum of a hybrid engine rolling up the driveway without headlights. Lucas's blood went cold. Nobody made house calls at midnight with their lights off unless they were up to no good.

The vehicle stopped near Amy's front porch, and Lucas heard a car door close. Heavy footsteps crossed the wooden boards, then there was an aggressive pounding on Amy's front door.

"Open up! I know you're in there!"

The voice was male, irate, and carried the kind of authority that expected immediate compliance. It was almost as though whoever was behind the pounding and the voice, was trying to catch her by surprise, hoping to frighten her. Lucas willed Amy to stay inside, not to answer the door, but within moments he heard her voice.

"It's late. Whatever you want can wait until morning."

"You have something I want, and I'm not leaving without it."

Rusty was on his feet now, hackles raised and a growl building in his chest. Lucas had never seen Rusty act like this. The dog recognized the threat even through the walls.

Lucas clutched his cane and made his way to his front door. Every instinct screamed that Amy was in danger. When he stepped onto his porch, he could see the scene clearly.

A man in a suit stood way too close to Amy as she stood in her doorway, leaning forward in a way that was clearly meant to intimidate. Amy was trying to maintain composure, but Lucas could see the fear in her posture.

"The bridle isn't here anymore," she was saying. "Even if I wanted to sell it to you, I couldn't."

"Don't lie to me!" Klaus Weber's voice rose to a shout.

"Amy isn't lying," Lucas called out, making his way carefully off his porch and up onto Amy's. "The bridle is gone. Please leave."

Klaus turned toward him with obvious contempt. "Well, well. The wounded Amish farmhand is going to rescue the lady." His laugh was ugly. "What are you going to do? Hit me with your walking stick? Your people don't fight. Everybody knows that."

Lucas positioned himself between Klaus and Amy, leaning heavily on his cane but standing as straight as his healing body would allow. "You're right. I don't believe in fighting. My religious beliefs keep me from using violence to solve anything. But Amy is telling the truth, the bridle is no longer here. We couldn't get it for you even if we tried."

"I don't believe you." Klaus stepped closer, his stocky bulk meant to intimidate.

"But the problem is," Lucas stood his ground, continuing to speak calmly. "Rusty here does not share my religious beliefs, because he's, well... a dog."

Rusty had placed himself slightly in front of Lucas, and the low growl became a snarl showing off every sharp tooth. In the darkness, all Klaus could see was eighty pounds of German Shepherd with bared fangs and the kind of focused attention that meant business.

"My dog sees a man threatening two people who helped save his life," Lucas said conversationally. "If I were you, I wouldn't make any sudden moves. You know how German Shepherds are. Loyal to the death. Vicious when necessary. Weren't they favorites of your *people?*"

Klaus took an involuntary step backward, his eyes fixed on Rusty's threatening posture. Not only were the dog's teeth bared, but he had lowered into a crouch showing he was ready to spring into action.

"What do you mean, 'your people?' I'm not German."

"I mean the kind who think they may intimidate women in the

middle of the night and take whatever they want. Those kinds of people."

Amy had disappeared from the doorway, and Klaus was too focused on the snarling dog to notice. When she reappeared, she was carrying Rick's shotgun. "Am I supposed to be intimidated?" Her voice was steady. "You need to get off my porch, Klaus. The bridle is in New York with people who know how to handle Nazi artifacts properly. I hope I never have to see it again."

Klaus looked from the shotgun to the dog to Lucas's calm expression, finally understanding that the situation had shifted out of his control.

"This isn't over," he said, backing toward his car.

"Yes, Klaus, it is," Amy replied. "Never step foot on my property again."

Klaus climbed into his hybrid and drove away—this time with his headlights on.

Brady emerged from his RV just as the taillights disappeared down the road. He took in the scene—Amy holding a shotgun, Lucas praising Rusty, the lingering tension in the air.

"Everything all right here?" he asked.

"Just fine," Amy said, lowering the shotgun. "Though I probably should have thought this gun thing through a little better."

"You don't even know how to load that thing, do you?" Brady observed.

"Nope," Amy admitted with a shaky laugh.

CHAPTER 20

Thirty minutes later, Officer Bob Powell from the Sugarcreek Police Department was sitting at my kitchen table, his notebook open as he documented Klaus Weber's midnight intimidation tactics.

"You did everything right," he assured us, accepting a cup of coffee from Brady. "Threatening behavior, trespassing, attempting to coerce a sale through intimidation—we might not have enough physical evidence to charge him, but we've got enough to bring him down to the police station for questioning if he surfaces again."

"Do you think he will?" I asked.

"Doubtful. Men like Weber rely on people being too scared or isolated to fight back. Once they realize you've got community support and law enforcement involved, they move on to easier targets."

"That's quite a dog," Officer Powell observed, glancing down at Rusty, lying peacefully at Lucas's feet. He hadn't growled or shown any concern over the cop sitting in my kitchen. "German Shepherds are known for their protective instincts. Weber probably didn't expect to face any kind of opposition from an Amish farmer."

"My daughter's no pushover, either," Brady said. "Except she needs to learn how to load a shotgun if she intends to point it at Weber again."

"Might not be a bad idea," Officer Powell agreed. "I can suggest a good gun safety class if you're interested. One of our former cops teaches it."

"I'll think about it."

After the officer left, I walked back into the kitchen and squatted down to scratch behind the ears of the dog Lucas had brought home.

"We needed a dog around the place and we didn't even know it." The dog closed his eyes with enjoyment as I continued to scratch and ruffle his fur. "Looks like I'll be picking up some nice dog treats today. You're a good dog, Rusty!"

CHAPTER 21

The morning sun continued to rise as I sat on the front porch steps, nursing a cup of coffee while I replayed Klaus Weber's threats in my head. I still felt a little nervous remembering the way he had stood at my door late last night, demanding the bridle even after I'd told him it was gone.

Brady emerged from the RV carrying his own mug. Without a word, he seated himself beside me on the narrow step, close enough that our shoulders touched.

"Sleep any last night?" he asked.

"Some." I took a sip of lukewarm coffee and grimaced.

Through the pasture, we could see Lucas working with Rusty on basic commands, both of them moving carefully but with obvious trust in each other.

"I was scared," I admitted. "Not for me—for Lucas. He's still healing, still using a cane, and there he was putting himself between me and that awful man."

Brady thought this over. "You really care about him."

"How can I not? He's been nothing but good to me since I got here.

I couldn't stand the thought of him getting hurt because of something I brought to his doorstep."

"It wasn't your fault Klaus showed up."

"Wasn't it? I'm the one who discovered the insignia, told Lucas about it in front of a couple of people at the hospital, then investigated it by asking Zelda to look at it. I'm the reason it attracted the wrong attention." I shook my head. "Lucas has been through enough without having to deal with problems I cause."

"Want some more coffee?" Brady offered. "I've got a fresh pot in the RV."

"Thanks, but I think this is going to have to be a one-cup day. My nerves are shot after last night."

"Suit yourself, but the offer stands," Brady said.

Watching Lucas working with Rusty was nice. There was something rich about sitting there in the early morning sunshine with my dad, watching the man I loved enjoy his new friend. I could hear Lucas's voice calling out, "Good dog!" as Rusty obediently put out a paw to shake.

"You know what I learned in prison?" Brady said. "Sometimes the worst thing you can do is try to carry everything alone. My preacher from back home drove all the way to the prison once a week to encourage me. That old man wasn't all that good in the pulpit—I slept through most of his sermons when I was a teenager—but he made a difference. He was good people, and that boy of yours strikes me as good people, too."

"Speaking of carrying things alone," I said, "I've been meaning to talk to you about the farm work. I know Lucas's Amish friends have been helping, but you've been doing so much, Brady. Lucas is slowly getting stronger, but he's nowhere near ready to handle everything himself."

"I don't mind the work."

"I appreciate that, but I also know you have your own life, your own career. I don't expect you to stay here indefinitely."

126

Brady took his time considering my words. When he finally spoke, he said, "Amy, I spent twenty-nine years not knowing I had a daughter. I had years of empty hotel rooms and arenas full of strangers. Sweetheart, my career involves not much more than facing bat-crazy bulls day after day who want to kill me. I spend a lot of time praying I can run faster, dodge quicker, and think smarter than all of them. Someday, maybe sooner than later, there will be one that is smarter and faster than me. You think I'm in a hurry to get back to that?"

The simple honesty in his voice made my throat ache.

He turned to look at me directly. "I'm not saying I'll stay forever. But right now, there's nowhere else in the world I'd rather be."

I threw my arm around his shoulder. "There's nowhere else in the world I'd rather you be, either."

We sat there like that for a while—just savoring the reality that we'd found each other. I took another sip of coffee.

"Your mother really did a number on both of us, didn't she," Brady said.

I nearly choked on my coffee. "That's putting it mildly."

"I keep thinking about that scared kid who showed up in our barn all those years ago. How different things might have been if I'd handled it better, if I'd somehow convinced her to stay."

"Brady, you can't blame yourself for her choices. I've spent my whole life watching her run from anything that required genuine commitment except for her career, and sometimes me."

"Still stings, though. Knowing she'd rather face Hollywood alone than build something real with people who loved her."

I thought about Desiree's pattern of dramatic entrances and exits, how she collected people like souvenirs but never seemed to actually keep them. "We both deserved better."

"We did. But you know what? We found each other anyway," Brady's voice warmed. "That's got to count for something."

Through the pasture, Lucas was heading back toward the house, Rusty trotting proudly beside him with a stick in his mouth.

"I've been thinking," Brady said. "Been meaning to find a church to be part of since I got out of prison, but never seemed to hang around anywhere long enough."

"I'm sorry."

"Found God behind bars, Amy. It wasn't exactly a Damascus Road experience, but it was real enough. Figured I ought to do something about it now that I'm staying in one place." He scratched his jaw thoughtfully. "I've heard good things about that Mennonite church over in Walnut Creek."

"Mennonite?" That was a shock. "Aren't they ultra-conservative? Don't the women all wear the same kinds of clothes as the Amish, along with head coverings?"

"I'm not sure, but what I've heard is that there's about as many kinds of Mennonite churches around here as there used to be Baptist churches back in Texas where I come from. Some are more conservative than others. All I need is some good preaching, some praying, and a song or two. One of Erma's granddaughters goes there and says you don't have to dress funny to show up.

The idea surprised me, but in a good way. "I might like to go with you, if you don't mind the company."

Brady's face lit up as if I'd given him the best gift imaginable. "Now, wouldn't that be something? My very own daughter sitting beside me in church. Can you imagine? Never thought I'd see the day."

The simple joy in his voice made me smile for the first time since Klaus Weber's visit. "It's a date, then."

"A date." Brady stood up, suddenly energized. "Better go help Lucas with whatever project he's working on. Man's been good to you, least I can do is make sure he doesn't overdo it while he's still healing."

As I watched him stride across the yard toward Lucas, I felt something warm in my chest. Maybe we couldn't undo all the damage Desiree had done, but we could build something new from what was left. Something real and lasting, built on showing up for each other when it mattered.

Some families were born. Others were built, one careful day at a time filled with kindness.

CHAPTER 22

Lucas had worked on Amy's leather bag all morning. It was laborious work, but he enjoyed it because it was for her. No one had seen it yet because he kept it on a table in his bedroom, covered over by a sheet when he wasn't working on it.

He was pleased with the design—a place for everything he could think of that she might need. Even a pocket to keep her wallet in if she wanted to. The image he was creating should make her happy. It certainly made him happy. So many memories. He could only work on it for a couple of hours, then he had to get up, stretch, and do something else or his back would seize up from the strain.

At the moment, he stood in front of the small mirror in his bathroom, running his fingers along the left side of his jaw where his beard was attempting to grow back. Nine weeks after the accident, most of the visible damage had healed, but the scar tissue along his jawline told a different story.

The beard grew unevenly now. The right side grew thick and dark as it always had, but the left side showed patches where facial hair would never grow again—places where surgeons had worked to repair damage from where he'd been dragged behind the runaway buggy. The result was a beard that looked unfinished, broken.

For an Amish man, a beard carried too much social weight to take lightly. It represented maturity, commitment to the community, and most times—marital status. Lucas had worn one since he had married at twenty-two and had grown accustomed to how it looked. It helped him blend seamlessly with other Amish men his age—which he valued. With the damaged version, he looked like he was caught between worlds.

The reflection looking back at him was of a man much thinner than he'd been in years, with lines around his eyes that spoke of pain and recovery. This patchy beard that marked him as obviously damaged—someone who'd been broken and put back together imperfectly—bothered him.

Lucas picked up the razor he'd kept from his teenage years—an impulsive purchase when he'd gotten his first paycheck from a carpentry job and wanted to buy something nice for himself. He hesitated, looking in the mirror, holding the razor in his hand.

"What do you think, Rusty?" he asked. "Is this a good idea?"

Rusty had been watching him from the spot on the bathroom floor he'd chosen for himself. Now he raised his head and barked once, then laid back down and closed his eyes.

"If that's a 'yes', I'll blame you if anyone complains."

Lucas eased the blade along his jawline, removing the patchy growth that made him feel like someone caught between identities. When he finished, his reflection revealed someone younger, more vulnerable. No longer hiding scars behind incomplete attempts at normalcy.

He touched his smooth jaw, studying this new version of himself. Without the beard, and without the bowl haircut—the hair on his head was still growing out from being shaved for the surgery—he could easily pass for *Englisch*. The thought should have left him appalled. Instead, to his chagrin, he felt something close to relief.

Some changes couldn't be entirely hidden, only accepted.

When he emerged clean-shaven from the bathroom, Rusty lifted his head and studied him with intelligent brown eyes.

"Well?" Lucas asked. "What's the verdict?"

Rusty stood, walked over, and bumped his nose against Lucas's hand. Approval, acceptance, or maybe just a request for breakfast. Regardless, what was done was done.

Outside, Amy was still working in the garden. Lucas wondered if she'd notice the change, and what she might think of it.

Maybe it was time to find out.

Lucas opened the screen door and followed Rusty outside onto the porch. A warm breeze from the gorgeous September day brushed his freshly shaved face in a way that felt foreign after years of beard coverage. The sensation was oddly liberating.

Amy kneeled between rows of late tomatoes, her back to him as she filled a basket with the season's last harvest. She wore an old work shirt that had seen better days and dirt-stained jeans, completely absorbed in her task.

He made his way down the porch steps, grateful his balance had improved to where he only needed the cane for stability rather than survival. Rusty trotted over and sniffed Amy's basket. She absent-mindedly patted the dog's head before plucking another tomato.

"Afternoon," Lucas said, stopping at the garden's edge.

"Afternoon," Amy replied without looking up, her hands continuing their efficient work among the vines. "These tomatoes are coming in better than I expected. Erma says we'll have enough for one more big canning for winter if—"

Her words died as she glanced over her shoulder. She blinked once, then turned fully to stare at him with the expression of someone trying to solve a puzzle.

"I'm sorry," she said politely, "but it seems you have me confused with someone else. I don't believe we've met."

Lucas felt his mouth twitch. "Amy."

"No, no. Amy is *my* name, but I'm not sure we've met before." She stood, brushing dirt from her knees while maintaining perfect composure. "You kind of look like the farmer who lives in my Daadi Haus." The only thing giving away her joke was the way the corners of her mouth were pinched—as though she was trying to stop from smiling.

"I shaved."

"Did you now?" She tilted her head, studying him with exaggerated curiosity. "And where exactly is Lucas? Because I'm fairly certain his sisters would notice if he'd been replaced by some clean-shaven stranger who happens to be wearing his clothes."

"Amy." He stepped closer, fighting a smile.

"Prove it," she said, crossing her arms. "Tell me something only Lucas would know."

He thought for a moment. "You're terrified of Zedekiah."

"Everyone knows that. Try again."

"You cry during thunderstorms but pretend you don't."

Her eyes narrowed. "Lucky guess. One more."

"You miss your mother—even though she drives you crazy."

"Go on."

"Last week you finished reading through the book of Revelation, and you asked more questions than a three-year-old."

"Which you did a pitiful job of answering."

"True."

"Well. I suppose you might actually be Lucas after all." She grinned and reached up to touch his smooth jaw with dirt-smudged fingers. "Though I have to say, this is quite the transformation. You look…"

"*Englisch?*"

"Different." Her touch lingered. "But still handsome enough to talk some unsuspecting Amish woman into marrying you, if you can find one who isn't related to you."

Lucas felt heat rise in his cheeks, but before he could come up with a response, Amy's smile grew mischievous.

"So, Mr. Clean-Shaven, what prompted this dramatic change? Please tell me it wasn't vanity. I'm pretty certain Amish men aren't allowed to be vain."

"The beard was growing unevenly. Made me look like someone who was half Amish and half *Englisch*."

"And have you decided which half you want to be?"

"I'm still figuring it out," he admitted.

Amy's breath caught. For a moment they stood there in the garden, surrounded by the ordinary sounds of farm life, while something shifted between them.

"Well," she said finally, her voice slightly unsteady. "I suppose I could get used to this new face."

"You approve?"

"I approve of the man wearing it." She picked up her basket of tomatoes. "Come on, stranger. Erma just got here. She's inside sterilizing canning jars. I'll make some tea, and we can hear all the news about her latest grandbaby. It was born last night, and she got to catch it."

CHAPTER 23

It had been over two weeks since Zelda had taken the bridle back to New York with her, and I hadn't heard a word. The deadline for her retirement from Sotheby's had passed. She had not called, and there had been no communication from Klaus after his midnight visit either. He had threatened me with a "you'll be sorry," as he left, but so far, so good.

Lucas had been consistently getting stronger. It was good to see him beginning to do a few chores around the farm. Brady began leaving some light chores specifically for him if he knew Lucas was strong enough to do them.

Everything was peaceful here. I'd always loved the fall, and September in the Sugarcreek area was especially lovely. I was feeling good about life and admiring the twenty-four quarts of ruby-red tomato juice Erma and I had just finished canning when that peace was shattered by the sound of an engine being pushed well beyond reasonable limits announcing the arrival of—I glanced out the window—a hurricane named Desiree.

She roared into the driveway in a red BMW convertible, like someone who'd spent thirty years making dramatic entrances, spraying gravel as she braked hard. Even from a distance, I could see her perfectly highlighted honey-blonde hair whipping in the wind, held back by what was most likely a silk Hermès scarf that probably cost more than my car payment.

"Looks like your mother has come for a visit," Lucas said, as he eased into his porch chair with the careful movements of someone still relearning the limits of his body.

"In all her dramatic glory." I watched her spring from the car as if she were entering a movie premiere rather than a farm in rural Ohio. "I've missed her."

Desiree enveloped me in a cloud of expensive perfume and theatrical emotion before I could properly brace myself. "Amy, darling! You look absolutely exhausted. Thank goodness I'm here now to help you."

She was dressed for a photo shoot rather than a visit with her daughter—white linen pants that would show every speck of dust, strappy sandals with three-inch heels completely inappropriate for graveled driveways, and oversized sunglasses. Everything about her screamed expensive, artificial, and utterly out of place.

"It's good to see you, Mom, but we're doing pretty well right now."

"Nonsense. A mother's place is with her daughter during a crisis." She turned her attention to Lucas with the bright, predatory focus of a spotlight finding its target. "Hello Lucas. You look so much better than I expected, considering the messages Amy left me. Goodness! You look very handsome without that beard!"

Lucas had already retreated into that polite, distant space he occupied whenever forced into Desiree's orbit. Her constant motion and energy seemed to exhaust him even during his good days.

"Thank you," he said, his response carefully neutral.

"Well, I hope you're taking proper care of yourself. Brain injuries are nothing to be trifled with, you know. I had a co-star once who—"

"Mom." I cut her off before she could launch into what would undoubtedly be a dramatic and largely fictional story about Hollywood medical emergencies. "What are you doing here? I thought you were still in Romania."

"Wrapped up early, thank heavens. The director was a tyrant, and the script was dreadful. I don't know what my agent was thinking, talking me into doing it. I need a nice, long rest somewhere peaceful." She gestured vaguely at the farm around us as if claiming it for her personal retreat. "I'm going to be staying with you for a while."

Before I could process the implications of "a while," Erma came walking toward us from the direction of the vegetable garden, carrying a basket of late tomatoes. She took one look at my mother and stopped dead in her tracks.

Then the basket of tomatoes hit the ground. Erma had not yet met my mother. Desiree had never stayed more than a few hours before.

I knew my mother could be a bit much for the people here in Sugarcreek, but I thought Erma's reaction was a bit more extreme than necessary.

"*Mein Gott,*" Erma whispered, staring at Desiree with wide eyes. "*Dorcas? Dorcas Schlabach?*"

The change in my mother was instantaneous and terrible. All the carefully cultivated poise, theatrical confidence, the commanding presence that had carried her through thirty years of Hollywood success drained away, leaving her looking smaller and more uncertain than I'd ever seen her.

"I'm sorry," Desiree said, her voice higher than usual. "I think you have me confused with someone else."

But Erma was walking closer, her expression growing more certain with each step. "*Du bischt Dorcas Schlabach. Amos un Hazel's dochter. Ich hab dich gekannt ven du varst yung.*"

I didn't understand the Pennsylvania Dutch, but I didn't need to. The recognition in Erma's voice, the growing panic in my mother's eyes—confirmed what Rick's letter had told me about Desiree's identity and upbringing.

"I don't know what you're talking about," Desiree said, backing away from Erma like the Amish woman was a ghost. "You've mistaken me for someone else."

"*Du bischt avek gerannt ven du varst siebetsen,*" Erma continued, her voice gentle but relentless. "Your parents, they never stopped looking for you. They died without knowing what happened to their little girl."

"I don't know who you think I am, Erma, but I am assuredly not that person."

Erma and I looked at each other, and then back at her. Erma had caught it, too.

"I never mentioned Erma's name to you, Mom. How do you know who she is?"

"Stop." Desiree's voice cracked like thin ice under pressure. "Both of you! Please, just stop."

But Erma didn't stop. She continued to talk to her in the Pennsylvania Dutch language.

I didn't know what Erma was saying, but it was really getting to Mom. She swayed on her heels, one hand gripping the porch railing for support.

Lucas was watching the scene unfold with careful attention. Erma had switched back to English, her voice thick with emotion.

"Your *mamm* and *daett*, they prayed for you every day. Every morning at breakfast, every evening before bed. They never gave up hope."

"You didn't know my father!" Desiree said, in a much louder voice than necessary—as though trying to drown Erma's words out. "You would have run away, too if you'd endured what I did."

"I knew your father, and I would not have wanted to be raised by him—but your *mamm* was kind and gentle. She never stopped believing you would come back someday."

"My *mamm* was weak," Desiree said bitterly. "She let him work me like a mule and punish me whenever he wanted."

"Your *mamm* was ill, but she loved you." Erma's eyes were bright with unshed tears. "Your *daett* sold the farm and took her to Mt. Hope, where they moved in with her family. He used the money from the sale of the farm to help take care of her. Now, both are buried in the cemetery. We can go see their graves. I'll go with you."

Desiree crumpled then, the careful facade destroyed by Erma's stubborn refusal to believe Desiree's lie. Now, she doubled over, holding her stomach, sobbing with the raw grief of someone confronting a loss she'd denied for too long. The sound was heart-breaking—not the theatrical weeping of one of her performances, but genuine anguish.

"I wanted to call, to write, to visit," she gasped between sobs. "I wanted to let them see their granddaughter, but I was afraid."

"What were you afraid of, Dorcas?"

It seemed strange to hear her called by this name.

"I was afraid that if *Daett* ever found out where I was, he'd send people to grab me and bring me home—whether or not I wanted to."

"You were on the big screen." I asked a question I'd wanted to ask ever since I'd read Rick's letter. "Didn't you think he'd hear about you?"

"I dyed my hair blonde, I got a nose job, got my teeth fixed, I wore eye makeup, I wore fine clothes. Besides, there was no way *Daett* would ever go to the movies."

Erma stepped forward and, without hesitation, gathered my mother into her arms. "*Ach*, little one. They just wanted to know that you were safe. That's all."

Standing there on the porch, watching my sophisticated mother fall apart in the arms of an Amish woman who had known her as a girl, I felt like I was seeing the real Desiree Stanton for the first time in my life. Not the actress, not the celebrity, not the drama queen who often left chaos in her wake. Just a scared, guilty daughter who had been running from her childhood most of her life.

I went to help Erma put my mother back together.

CHAPTER 24

I was still trying to process the sight of my mother sobbing in Erma's arms when the sound of Brady's truck pulling into the driveway caught my attention. He'd just returned from a quick run to town, and his timing couldn't have been worse.

Brady climbed out of his pickup, whistling slightly off-key, like he always did when he was in a good mood. He'd been to the feed store and the hardware store, and I could see bags of horse supplement and coils of new fence wire in the truck bed.

A normal afternoon on a normal day, except nothing about this day was turning out to be normal.

He looked up toward the porch, probably expecting to see me or Lucas. Instead, he saw a red BMW convertible parked like it owned the yard, Erma comforting a weeping stranger in fancy clothes, and me standing next to them trying to help.

Brady stopped walking.

From his angle, he couldn't see Desiree's face clearly—my mother's head was buried against Erma's shoulder. But something about the scene made him go still, the way he did in the rodeo arena when he sensed a bull was about to charge.

"Amy?" His voice carried a careful note of concern. "Everything all right here?"

Desiree must have heard his voice, because she went rigid in Erma's arms. She pulled back slowly and turned toward the sound.

The effect was immediate and devastating. Brady's face cycled through emotions I'd never seen him display—shock, recognition, disbelief, and then something that looked like physical pain.

When he finally spoke, his voice held a note of resignation. "Darla." It was as though he had been expecting this moment his whole life and wasn't happy it had finally arrived.

The name that Desiree had been using when she first met Brady made her go pale as a ghost. She staggered backward, one hand covering her mouth, her eyes round and wide with shock.

He took a step closer, and I saw his hands clench into fists at his sides. He'd told me he had forgiven her—but I thought he was probably wrong about that. What I saw now was twenty-nine years of carefully controlled anger beginning to leak out around the edges.

Lucas had been silent, but now he cleared his throat. "Brady..." he cautioned.

Brady looked at him as if just now realizing there were other people present. He glanced around, taking in our small audience.

Erma watched with the careful neutrality of someone who'd seen plenty of family drama over the years.

Brady focused on my mom again. "It's good to see you after all these years, Darla. I think it's time we had us a little talk."

"Brady, please—" Desiree started. Then she turned to me. "This is all *your* fault. If I'd known he was here, I wouldn't have come! Why didn't you tell me?"

"If you'd ever bothered to call ahead and let me know you were coming, I would have!" The words came out a little more forcefully than I had intended.

"I will not hurt you, Darla, or Desiree, or whatever you're calling yourself these days. I never laid a hand on you when we were married, and I never will. You know that. Let's go to my RV where we can talk. I've got a few questions stored up—and I'd like some answers before you disappear again." He started walking toward where his RV was parked, his stride long and determined.

Desiree gave a dramatic sigh—then, after a moment's hesitation, followed, stumbling slightly in her heels.

We watched them disappear into the RV, Brady's shoulders rigid with suppressed rage, Desiree trailing behind him like someone walking to her own execution.

"Well," Erma said, "this is going to be interesting."

She was right. Even from this distance, we could hear the first explosion of voices from Brady's RV—his deep rumble of accumulated grievances, her high-pitched responses. The words were indistinct, but the emotions were clear enough.

Lucas shifted uncomfortably in his chair as the voices went on and on. "Should we do something...?"

"No," I said firmly. "This is thirty years overdue. They need to get their words out."

The voices from the RV rose and fell like a thunderstorm.

"Poor little Dorcas," Erma plopped into the porch chair beside Lucas. Apparently, she had no intention of leaving. "I remember her as a girl. Smart as a whip. Pretty as a flower. And wild as a March hare, that one. Her *daett* was a harsh man. He used to work her half to death. I saw her come in from the fields, her face peeling from sunburn, and her fingers bleeding from clawing rocks out of the earth so his plow wouldn't catch on them. That was just one job he gave her."

"Besides hard work, was she physically abused?" I asked.

"We suspected it," Erma said. "We had no proof and no one to tell even if it were true. He was one of those fathers who liked to quote the 'spare the rod and spoil the child' scripture a lot. He never seemed to notice the warning in the Bible about fathers not provoking their children to wrath. Dorcas was one angry teenager before she left. I didn't blame her much. I wouldn't have wanted to be raised by him."

A loud crash came from the direction of the RV—something thrown or dropped hard.

"Should we check on them?" Lucas asked.

"They're adults," I said, although I wasn't entirely convinced. "They can work it out."

"Or kill each other," Erma observed mildly.

"Don't worry." Brady stuck his head out the door. "Darla knocked over the microwave, but she didn't mean to."

Another crash. Brady stuck his head out again. "That was the TV... I'm sure she didn't mean to break that either!" He slammed the door shut. Then silence.

At this rate, they were going to need either a bigger RV or smaller emotions.

The silence was worse than the shouting and the two crashes.

"Maybe I should—" I started.

"Give them time," Erma said firmly. "Wounds need to be washed out before they can heal."

We waited for several minutes, listening for sounds from the RV. Even the farm seemed to hold its breath. The chickens weren't clucking, Zedekiah wasn't crowing.

Time passed while I stared at Brady's RV and wondered if my parents were going to emerge speaking to each other or if one or both of them were going to need medical attention.

"You know," Erma said thoughtfully, "over the years, I've learned that sometimes love and hurt can get so tangled up together you can't separate one from the other. Maybe that's what they're doing in there —trying to untangle thirty years' worth of knots."

"What if they can't untangle them?" I asked.

"Then at least they'll know they tried."

As if summoned by her words, the RV door opened. Brady

emerged first. He looked lighter, like a man who'd finally set down a weight he'd been carrying too long.

Desiree followed a moment later, moving slowly. Her perfect makeup was gone, her face and eyes puffy from crying, her hair a hot mess—her scarf was crumpled into a ball in one hand as though she might have used it as a handkerchief. Her shoes were off. She held them in the other hand by their heels.

Frankly, she looked at least ten years older than when she had first arrived. It was startling to see her actual age showing.

Brady said something to her we couldn't hear. She nodded and walked barefoot across the yard toward us.

I whispered to Erma. "At least they're both alive."

"I got the fence material we needed," Brady told Lucas. "You want to come help."

"Sure do." Lucas grabbed his cane and made his way down the porch steps toward the truck, obviously eager to get away. Rusty followed him, and Brady lifted him into the bed of the truck. If I could have gotten away with it, I would have rather mended fences, too.

"Are you okay?" I asked my mother.

"No. I'm most certainly not," Desiree said.

"What do you need?" I asked. "How can I help?"

"I need two Tylenol capsules, a shower, a cup of hot tea, and a bed. Then, I intend to pull the covers over my head and sleep until I don't want to sleep anymore. After that, I might consider talking to Brady again. Maybe. At the moment, never seeing him again as long as I live seems a much more appealing choice."

147

CHAPTER 25

"I have good news, and I have bad news," Zelda's crisp voice over the phone carried no preliminaries or hint of humor. "Which do you want first?"

I turned the phone on speaker and set it in the middle of my kitchen table so Lucas could also hear. "Tell me the good news first."

"Rick's situation is resolved. I returned his items to inventory, wrote it up as a clerical error, and everyone is happy. This isn't the first time something got lost and was discovered years later."

My relief was immediate. One crisis handled, at least.

"Now, about the bridle," Zelda continued. "I've had it examined by Dr. Heinrich Kessler from the Austrian Cultural Heritage Institute. That took a while, which is why you haven't heard from me these past two weeks. The leatherwork is distinctive. It has a particular style, as I suspected, used only at a certain riding school in Vienna."

"So, it is definitely Austrian?"

"Yes. It was crafted by master artisans for the imperial program." Zelda's voice took on the focused tone I could imagine her using during academic lectures. "Dr. Kessler believes it's connected to a famous rescue mission in 1945 that evacuated the Lipizzaner horses from Czechoslovakia."

"I thought you said it was Austrian."

"I did. The horses had originally been evacuated from Vienna, Austria, to protect them from Allied bombing. They were moved to the Hostau stud farm in Czechoslovakia, which was then under German occupation. Apparently, a few of the German officers involved with the horses had the eagle/swastika insignia inscribed on the surviving bridles."

"Weird," I said.

"It was a strange time," Zelda agreed. "And a dangerous one for horses and people. When the war drew to a close in the spring of 1945, the horses became trapped at Hostau between advancing Soviet forces from the east and retreating German forces in the west. There was genuine concern the horses would be killed in the fighting or slaughtered for food by the Russian soldiers when they arrived."

"Food!"

"The troops were starving. They'd done it before."

I grimaced. "Go on."

"American forces conducted something they called Operation Cowboy to rescue the horses and bring them safely to American-controlled territory in Germany, and eventually back to Austria where they belonged. Some German officers contacted General George Patton and asked for his help in coordinating an evacuation. In return, they promised to surrender and allow themselves to be taken as prisoners. If the plan failed, they could have been killed as traitors, but they loved the horses and couldn't bear to see them destroyed."

I felt a flicker of hope. This sounded like heroism instead of the horrors I had been imagining.

"The quality and craftsmanship of this bridle suggest it may have belonged to a high-ranking German officer. Someone with significant authority in the program."

"Which means?"

"Which means the Austrian ministry wants to investigate its provenance. They're making inquiries at various international agencies—genealogy databases, displaced person's records, immigration documents." Her voice grew more serious. "Amy, this bridle is unique. If it belonged to some German officer who emigrated to America, there will be official questions asked."

"Wouldn't whoever owned it be too old to still be a danger?"

"Of course, but it isn't a matter of danger. It's a matter of justice. For instance, three years ago a former concentration camp guard was discovered and prosecuted. He was one hundred and one years old."

Lucas and I exchanged glances.

"One hundred and one?" I said. "Seriously?"

"Seriously." Zelda gave a sigh, presumably at my ignorance. "But apart from that, it is of historical significance. Many war criminals simply disappeared into the US and embedded themselves in various communities. One of the worst war criminals lived in the Detroit area for years. He grew a garden and gave tomatoes to his neighbors. The neighbors said he was just the nicest guy. No one had any idea they were living next door to an important member of the Nazi's Death Head Battalion—who were among the worst of the worst."

"I understand, but we don't have any knowledge to give anyone. The only thing we can honestly say is that Lucas found it in a box of junk at a local thrift store!"

"The Austrians will try to find some historical documentation, regardless. Who owned it, how it came to America, whether there are living relatives who might have information about its wartime significance."

"Oh dear," I said. "This isn't going away, is it?"

"Which brings up my next point." Her voice carried a note of compassion. "Would you have room for a houseguest? It might be best if I were there to help you deal with the investigation. That would be better accomplished if I were on site."

I looked around my kitchen, thinking about Desiree in the guest room, Brady in his RV, the two of them trying to avoid each other, and now the possibility of Zelda joining our strange household.

"I have another guest room, and you are welcome to it. But, Zelda, you should know that my mother is here. She's... an actress. We're still working through some complicated family issues."

"I've met your mother." Zelda sounded amused. "I'm sure my visit will be delightfully theatrical if she's visiting there. I've dealt with high-strung art collectors for years. I think I can handle one performer."

"If you say so." I had my doubts. "When could you get here?"

"I'm already packed. I'll arrive tonight."

After she disconnected, Lucas and I sat for a moment, processing what we'd learned.

"So, we know it's connected to a horse rescue operation," I said finally. "That's good news."

"But we still don't know how it ended up in Sugarcreek. Or who the high-ranking officer was." Lucas grabbed an oatmeal cookie from a plate of homemade ones Erma had left. "I guess this will teach me not to go to thrift stores in the future. No telling what you might find there or what trouble it might cause."

CHAPTER 26

The first thing I did was prepare Zelda's room. Fresh bed linens, a vase of flowers from the garden, a light dusting. I'd done little to the house since I'd inherited it. Rick had good taste, and I'd seen no need to change anything. Now that I was staying here indefinitely, perhaps I'd spruce things up a little—but not today.

Mom wandered out of her bedroom, went to the bathroom, and when I tried to speak to her, she held up her hand, palm out, letting me know she was not ready to be spoken to yet. She disappeared back into the bedroom and locked the door.

Next thing on the agenda was groceries.

On my way to the grocery store, I stopped in at the Harvest Thrift store to give them my phone number in case they came across a clue as to who might have dropped off that box of old bridles that had turned our lives upside-down.

It felt a little strange not having a writing project hanging over me. I had worked so hard these past few years to support myself with my writing, I rarely had any extra time. In fact, I often had to set an alarm while working just to remind myself to stand up and walk around so my body wouldn't atrophy. I hadn't wandered around a thrift store in ages. Or wandered around *any* store, for that matter.

Besides, with an entire antique store filled with Rick's acquisitions, I didn't have any need or desire to purchase anything—but then I saw the walking cane.

It was handmade of twisted wood, the kind I'd heard referred to as a snake stick because it resembled the winding nature of a snake. Someone had polished it to a lovely sheen. The price was low considering the time that had been invested in it, but I thought Lucas might be ready for something like this instead of his crutches or three-pronged cane. Maybe he'd enjoy trying it.

When I took my selection to the counter to purchase it, I mentioned the box of old bridles to the woman at the counter, hoping she'd remember something. The only thing she remembered was the same thing Lucas had been told—someone had brought boxes and left them beside the door in the middle of the night.

While we were talking, another Mennonite volunteer overheard our conversation. She looked up from the quilts she was sorting nearby.

"Are you talking about those horse bridles? We've had more donations from the same man recently—only this time he came during regular hours." She folded a small baby quilt with careful precision. "His name is David Yoder, and he brought a whole truckload of boxes and stayed to chat while he rested. Poor soul seemed exhausted."

I moved closer to the quilt display, curious. "What did he say?"

"His father had died recently, and his mother went to live with his one remaining sister." The volunteer shook her head sympathetically. "He's cleaning out the homeplace all by himself so it can be sold. You could tell it was wearing on him—emotionally and physically."

"*Englisch* or Amish?" I asked, though I suspected I already knew the answer.

"Very *Englisch* now." Her voice carried a note of sadness. "But most of the things he's bringing are Amish. Such a pity."

"Why is that such a pity?"

The volunteer glanced around as if making sure no one else could hear. "He was raised Amish but left the church years ago. There was a shunning involved." She lowered her voice even further. "Now he's stuck dealing with all his family's belongings alone. A man in his seventies shouldn't have to carry that burden by himself, but his situation makes it complicated for others to help."

My heart went out to this stranger. "Yoder is such a common name around here. There must be dozens of David Yoders. Do you know where he lives now?"

"I don't know his current address, but I know the farm where he grew up. It's close to my parents' place." She reached for a scrap of paper from behind the counter. "I can draw you a map if you'd like. There's a big 'For Sale' sign out front—you can't miss it."

CHAPTER 27

I slowed when I reached the farm with the faded For Sale sign, immediately spotting an elderly man struggling with something heavy on the front porch. Sweat beaded on his forehead as he wrestled with what looked like an old treadle sewing machine, his face red with exertion and frustration.

Without thinking, I pulled into the driveway and got out. "Need a hand?"

Relief flooded his features. "Yes! These old Singer machines weigh more than they look."

Together, we maneuvered the ornate iron base through the doorway and onto the porch. Up close, I could see the beautiful craftsmanship—mother-of-pearl inlays, delicate scrollwork.

"My mother's," he explained, wiping his forehead with a handkerchief. "Ninety-five years old and still insisting she doesn't need help with anything. Took both of us to convince her to move in with my sister after her stroke."

He stuck his hand out to shake. "David Yoder. And before you ask —no, I'm not Amish anymore. Haven't been for so many years, my mother and sister quit shunning me after my dad passed."

The bitterness in his voice was unmistakable, but it was quickly replaced by obvious pride. "My grandson's coming tomorrow to help load the rest. That boy's strong as an ox—plays football for Ohio State! Straight A's too. Scholar *and* athlete."

His chest swelled as he talked about the boy, and I understood. Here was a man who'd been shunned for leaving the church, whose own relationship with his Amish father had been complicated, now living vicariously through a grandson who represented everything he'd hoped education could provide.

"Why don't you just auction the whole place off?" I asked, looking at the overwhelming accumulation. "Seems like it would be easier than doing all this yourself."

"That would be nice, but the problem is, auction houses want the good stuff and leave you with all the junk. Plus, they take forty percent right off the top." He gestured toward the cluttered outbuildings. "And that's assuming I can get them to come out here for what might be a bunch of worthless farm castoffs."

He added more softly, "Besides, these were my parents' things. Feels wrong letting strangers rifle through their whole life, you know? Bad enough I have to do it myself."

The pain in his voice made me understand. This wasn't just about clearing out a house—it was about dismantling the physical evidence of a family that had been fractured by his decision to leave the church over forty years ago.

He looked familiar to me, and it finally came to me where I'd seen him. The son of the old woman who sat vigil with Lucas's family in the hospital. The woman I'd given up my seat to. He didn't seem to recognize me, which was just as well.

"Mr. Yoder," I said carefully, "I need to ask you about something. My name is Amy Stanton, and I found something unusual in a box of horse tack that was donated to the thrift store. The person there thought it might have come from your family's donation."

"What kind of something?" David's expression grew wary.

"A bridle. Very old, with fancy leatherwork, and silver fittings. When I cleaned it, I discovered some symbols engraved on the metalwork."

David considered this. "I threw a lot of old tack into boxes. Dirty, cracked pieces of leather. I didn't notice any special markings on anything."

"Do you think your father might have had any dealings with Nazis in WWI or II?"

David barked out a laugh.

"Why is that funny?"

"If you had known my dad, you wouldn't ask. Most upstanding Amish man you could ever ask for. The idea of his having anything to do with Nazism is ridiculous." He gestured around the farm. "But trying to clean this place up is like going on an archeological dig. Dad never threw anything away. Seventy years of farm auctions, estate sales, neighbors cleaning out barns—if it was old and interesting, he'd buy it or trade for it. If there were no room for it, he'd build another storage shed on the property. He'd bid on box lots without even looking at everything inside, just because the price was right."

I followed his gaze, seeing his family's farm with fresh eyes. Outbuildings stuffed with decades of accumulation, piles of "someday I'll fix that" projects.

"I've been at this for two months," David continued. "Every day I come here and fill another truck with stuff I can't identify and don't have room to store. That box you're talking about—" He shook his head. "I threw every piece of horse tack on the place into it just to get it out of my way."

"So, you don't remember the specific bridle?"

"I don't remember half of what I've hauled out of here," David said. "My back's shot, my patience is gone, and every day I find another box full of God-knows-what that Dad collected over the years."

"Noone in the family wants anything?"

He leaned against the porch railing, showing every one of his seventy-plus years. "My only son lives in California and couldn't care less about the family farm. My grandson has his whole life ahead of him—college, football, whatever comes after. My sister's four children are grown and living their own lives. None of them wants to be stuck with an old man's collection of other people's castoffs."

It was disappointing, but it looked like David Yoder and the farm he was cleaning out were a dead end.

CHAPTER 28

When I got home, my mom was in full hippie mode. That happened from time to time with her, and it was always a little disconcerting. Sometimes after a critical review, or a nasty breakup, Mom would retreat into a different persona and go dreamy and floaty for a while.

As I headed into the house, Mom was all natural-looking hair, bare feet, long skirts, minimal makeup, and was snapping fresh green beans on the porch. Somehow, in my absence, she'd turned Zedekiah into an admirer. He was sitting on the swing tucked up beside her, looking so happy I didn't know whether to laugh or cry. I'd really tried to befriend that bird, but he continued to hate me.

"Is there no man in the world you can't charm?" I asked.

"I'm sure there's one or two," she joked, stroking Zedekiah's head with one finger. He closed his eyes in ecstasy. "How did things go?"

I leaned against the banister near the swing. Zedekiah opened an eye and gave me an evil stare. I scooted a couple of feet farther away.

There hadn't been much time to tell Mom about the bridle and all that had transpired. I caught her up and then explained what had happened today while I was gone.

"I discovered where the donation to the thrift store came from, but it was a dead end. Just the home of an old Amish man who liked to go to auctions and farm sales. His son was cleaning up the place so he could sell it."

"You're a smart girl. I know you'll figure it out," Mom said. "If you're hungry, I made biscuits while you were gone and opened a fresh jar of strawberry jam. It should keep you from getting too hungry until supper's ready. There's ham in the oven, and I'll have potatoes and green beans to go with it."

As far as I was concerned, if it helped her to drift around my farm barefoot, wearing flowers in her hair, that was fine with me. She'd worked hard and deserved a little R&R. For the time being, the media didn't seem to know she was here—or didn't care anymore.

I knew from experience she would eventually snap out of it, but I hoped not right away. I liked Dreamy Mom a lot better than Drama Mom. Dreamy Mom cooked and told me I was smart. Drama Mom wanted me to stand up straight and dye my hair so I could attract a man.

"This reminds me of what she was like back when she first showed up at our farm down in Texas," Brady said later as he watched Desiree in the garden, picking the late summer squash. "That poor little thing. She was just a kid, but she'd somehow hitchhiked all the way to Texas and ended up in our barn. I found her asleep, curled up in the hay like a newborn colt."

Now, my mom was dressed in a simple off-the-shoulder blue sundress, her hair in a messy bun on top of her head and her face and shoulders kissed by the sun. The long sleep, and the few hours alone here on my farm today, had been good for her. She was glowing with either health or great body lotion—I couldn't tell which—and my father couldn't take his eyes off her, which I feared might be the point.

I wondered what had happened to her latest love interest, Phillipe-the-hotelier, and why he hadn't shown up yet. The last time she visited me, she'd flown in on Phillipe's private jet and was rhapsodizing about him.

I hadn't been home long when no-nonsense Zelda Bloom pulled into my driveway and climbed out of her rental with lots of luggage in the back. She intended to stay awhile, and I couldn't be happier.

I had not yet told anyone except Mom about my conversation with David Yoder earlier. It was just as well. I could give the details to everyone else at once.

Zelda seemed unusually pensive, so I didn't want to immediately tell her the disappointing information about the bridle. I thought she might need to relax after her journey for a bit. It turned out that relaxing was for other people—not Zelda.

She even waved away my offer of food or drink. She arrived ready to work. Without even allowing me to show her to her room, she dropped her luggage, sat down at the kitchen table, booted up her laptop and turned it around to face me. "Here's an email I think you should see, Amy."

The sender's name was Nolan Blackwood. The email address was from "Historical Truth Blog." The subject line read, "Research Inquiry - Sugarcreek Area WWII Artifact."

Dr. Bloom,

I'm a freelance journalist with a 500,000-listener podcast following. Lately, I've been researching and reporting on Nazi war criminals who embedded themselves into America in the years after WWII.

Reputable sources recently shared with me that you turned over some German military memorabilia in your possession—specifically a ceremonial SS bridle connected to the royal Lipizzaner stallions—now in the hands of an auction house.

I am creating a podcast entitled "Hidden History: Nazi Artifacts in Amish Country." It will air in two weeks. I believe the public has a right to know about these discoveries and their implications.

I would welcome the opportunity to interview you for this story. Please contact me as soon as you can to discuss your cooperation.

If I don't hear from you within the next ten days, I'll proceed with the podcast based on the information I've already gathered.

Sincerely, Nolan Blackwood: Historical Truth Blog

My coffee mug hit the table harder than I'd intended, sending liquid sloshing over the rim onto the table. I ran to grab a dish towel to wipe it up while my mind processed what I'd just read.

Multiple sources. Nazi artifacts. Amish Country. Publication is in two weeks.

"What's going on?" I exploded. "Implications? *What* implications?"

"I think this is Klaus Weber's way of getting back at you for handing the bridle over to Sotheby's instead of him." Zelda turned her laptop back around to face her. "As far as implications, during both world wars, many people viewed the Amish and Mennonites with suspicion and anger—especially those who had sacrificed sons and daughters to the war effort. They looked at the Amish, at their German heritage, their continued use of a Germanic language, and their pacifist stance and concluded their loyalties were not with America, but with Germany."

"You've got to be kidding!"

"I never kid," she informed me. "They were wrong, of course. The Amish people's loyalties were firmly where they had always been—to God, their families, and their churches. But if these are the implications to which Mr. Blackwood is referring, his podcast could stir up anti-Amish attitudes yet again—at least among some."

"Five hundred thousand followers for a podcast is significant," Desiree said from her cozy corner, where she sat demurely working on her knitting. I'd never seen her knit in my life.

I forced my attention back to the conversation with Zelda. What Nolan was proposing was exactly what our community did not need —unwanted attention from people who didn't understand or care about the delicate dynamics of a community like Sugarcreek. Two sensationalized and poorly written television series had caused enough damage—making a mockery of these people I cared deeply about.

The good people of Sugarcreek were far from perfect, but they did not deserve to be used as clickbait.

CHAPTER 29

"I found out something today," I said, as we were enjoying the meal Mom had prepared for us.

Zelda sat across from me with her reading glasses perched on her nose, looking every inch the academic. Lucas occupied the chair beside Zelda. Brady sat beside me, still wolfing down the excellent ham Mom had made. My mother drifted around, wearing her sundress, looking like she'd stepped out of a folk song.

"What kind of something?" Zelda asked, her voice sharp with attention.

"I met the person who dropped off the box at Harvest Thrift—the one that contained the bridle."

Suddenly, I had everyone's attention. I hated that what I had to tell them was so disappointing.

"I went to the thrift store today to see if they remembered anything about that box of tack Lucas bought. Long story, but they connected me with the man who donated it. His name is David Yoder. He knew nothing about the bridle. He says his father must have picked it up at a farm auction or something."

"David Yoder?" Lucas grew visibly agitated. "Seventies? *Englisch*?"

"Yes, why?"

"Where did you meet him?"

"His father's farm, out on Route 93," I said. "Did I do something wrong?"

"No," Lucas said. "You did nothing wrong, but if that is the David Yoder I'm thinking of—he's Bishop Elmer Yoder's son."

"Wait. What?" I stared at him, the pieces slowly coming together. "He said his father had passed away and his mother had moved in with his sister. He was getting the farm ready to sell. He complained a little about all the things his father had accumulated..."

"That's Elmer's son," Lucas said. "The bishop loved going to estate sales and farm auctions."

"Did this David Yoder know where his father got it?" Zelda asked, pulling out a pen and notebook.

"He didn't know," I said. "He just said his father threw nothing away, and he was worn out from trying to sort through decades of stuff no one in the family wanted."

"So, this Nolan Blackwood is going to make a big deal over a few scraps of leather an old Amish man bought at an auction somewhere," Brady said. "People aren't going to buy into that load of garbage."

"Actually, quite a few will do exactly that," Mom said, turning away from the counter where she was cutting slices from the delicious-looking German chocolate cake she'd baked.

When Desiree got into a role, she really got into it.

"What do you mean?" Brady asked.

I saw a flash of the sharp intelligence that had carried my mom through three decades in Hollywood. She was coming out of her hippie fog.

"What I mean is that I've spent thirty years learning how media works, and this Nolan Blackwood person has all the ingredients for the perfect story." Desiree's transformation was startling—from earth-mother to calculating professional in the space of a sentence. "Nazi artifacts discovered in peaceful Amish community? If he markets it well, he could double his podcast audience. Many people love hearing dirt about anyone who tries to stand for something. It makes them feel better about themselves."

"So, you think he'll pursue this regardless of any actual facts," Zelda observed, looking at her with fresh interest.

"Facts don't matter if the narrative is compelling enough." Desiree began pacing, her bare feet silent on the kitchen tiles, her long dress swishing around her ankles, the cake-cutting knife clasped in her right hand. "Conspiracy theories spread because they're simple and dramatic, and people love to be shocked, especially if the news doesn't directly impact them."

"So what can we do?" Brady asked.

"We get ahead of the story. Tell it ourselves before Blackwood can spin it his way." Desiree turned to face us, and I saw the strategic mind that had successfully navigated Hollywood politics. "But we need something more compelling than just 'the good bishop bought it by accident.' That's not exciting enough to compete with Nazi conspiracy theories."

"What kind of story *would* be compelling enough?" Lucas frowned. "Something we would have to make up? The bishop buying it by accident is probably exactly what happened."

"We need to give them the human story. Not just what happened to the bridle, but who it belonged to originally. Where it came from, how it ended up at whatever sale Bishop Elmer attended." Desiree's eyes were bright with the kind of energy I'd only seen when she was discussing a challenging role. "We need to trace its history."

"But how?" I asked. "David Yoder doesn't remember, and Bishop Elmer is gone."

"What about his widow?" Lucas suggested. "Jane Yoder. She's in her nineties, but her mind is still good."

"She might remember where her husband bought the bridle since it is so distinctive," Zelda said, glancing up from her notes. "It's a long shot, but it wouldn't hurt to ask."

"I've heard that Jane was an excellent rider when she was young," Lucas said. "If Bishop Elmer had brought home something as fancy as that bridle, she would have noticed it."

I felt a spark of hope.

"That could lead us to the original owner," Zelda said, her voice gaining excitement. "If we can document the bridle's actual history, show how it accidentally ended up in this community, we undercut any conspiracy theories—and the Austrian government would appreciate us doing whatever we can."

"Instead of 'Mysterious Nazi Artifacts Appear in Amish Country,'" Desiree said, "we get 'Local Family Unknowingly Preserves a Piece of Wartime History.' Much better story."

Brady was watching Desiree with an expression I couldn't quite read, but it looked a lot like respect. "You think this approach will work?"

"I think it's our best shot," she said. "But we need to move fast. This Nolan Blackwood gave Zelda a deadline. We can't waste time."

"But will Jane Yoder be willing to talk to us?" I gathered up the supper plates and took them to the sink. "Bishop Elmer hasn't been gone all that long, and bringing up her deceased husband's possessions might be upsetting."

"Not necessarily," Lucas said. "I've noticed that some widows and widowers welcome the chance to talk about their deceased spouse. It hurts when people avoid ever mentioning them. Ask Erma to arrange it. She's good friends with Jane and her daughter. If anyone could convince Jane to talk with us, it would be Erma."

"I'll call her," I said, reaching into my jeans pocket for my cell phone.

As I dialed, I hoped that a ninety-five-year-old woman's memory might miraculously hold the key to this mystery.

"Erma?" As usual, her answering machine clicked on. It was rare for her to answer since she was a busy woman and didn't spend a lot of time sitting in her phone shanty. "It's Amy. We need your help."

It was a long shot, but hopefully, we'd find out what Jane Yoder remembered about a bridle her husband brought home, possibly years ago.

Erma called me back within the hour, after talking with Jane's daughter, Barbara.

"Jane is willing to see you, but there are conditions."

I grabbed a pen and paper. "What kind of conditions?"

"You are to come tomorrow morning, no later than ten o'clock. Barbara says her mother is sharpest in the mornings, and after her ministroke, she tires easily by afternoon." Erma paused. "Also, Barbara wants the visit to be brief."

"Of course. We'll be respectful."

"And just you and Lucas. Too many people will overwhelm her."

After I thanked her and hung up, I found Lucas on his front porch, working through his evening physical therapy exercises. The routine had become second nature to him now—careful stretches, balancing work, and strengthening exercises that were slowly returning him to something approaching his former capabilities. He was removing the walking cast for longer periods of time now.

"We can see Jane Yoder tomorrow morning," I said. "But Barbara wants it kept short. And only the two of us. She's afraid more people would be overwhelming to her."

"That's reasonable." Lucas finished his final set of leg lifts before reaching for his cane. "I like Jane. She's always been kind to me, even when her husband was sometimes less understanding."

"Do you think she'll remember anything useful about the bridle?"

"If anyone would, it would be Jane. She notices things, always has. If Bishop Elmer brought something that unusual home, and she saw it, she would have paid attention."

"Let me ask you something else," I said. "Something personal."

"Okay." He looked a little wary.

"Do you like your cane?"

"It gets the job done." He stared at the three-pronged cane he'd been using. "But not particularly."

"Do you think you might like this one better?" I took the hand-whittled cane I'd gotten from the thrift store from behind my back and handed it to him.

"Oh!" He held it up and admired it. "If a man had to use a cane, this would be the one I'd choose!"

"It's yours."

He gave it a little twirl and smiled. "Much better!"

CHAPTER 30

The next morning, we drove to the small house where Jane Yoder now lived with her daughter. It was a tidy place, with a carefully tended garden and the peaceful orderliness that I so often noticed in the area. Amish women loved their flowers and gardens.

Barbara met us at the door, her small frame carrying the quiet dignity I'd come to associate with Amish women of her generation. She had the kind of understated strength that came from decades of managing households, raising children, running small businesses, and weathering life's storms without complaint or drama. But there was worry in her eyes.

"She didn't sleep well last night, and she's been nervous and asking about you ever since I told her you were coming," Barbara said, leading us through a living room filled with handmade furniture and the soft light of September morning sun. "But please, if she seems tired or confused, you'll need to go."

"We understand," I said.

Jane Yoder sat in a rocking chair by the front window, her nearly century-old body appearing translucent in the morning light. She looked like fine china that had been handled with love for generations

—delicate but unbroken, her pale blue eyes still sharp with intelligence.

A small child, perhaps eighteen months old, lay curled against her chest, his dark hair visible above a small quilt. Her white hair was pinned back neatly beneath her white prayer *kapp*, her hands moving in gentle, comforting circles upon the sleeping child's back.

"*Mamm*," Barbara said softly, "Amy and Lucas are here to see you."

Jane's eyes, still remarkably clear despite her age, focused on Lucas first. "You look well. I've prayed for you often since the accident."

"*Danki*, Jane. I'm grateful to be healing."

"Why are you carrying my husband's cane?"

"This was Elmer's?" Lucas held it up and inspected it. "I thought it looked familiar. Here, Jane, you can have it back."

"No, it would give Elmer pleasure to know you have it instead of some stranger. Our son, David, whittled it for him when he was just a teenager."

"I found it at the thrift store," I explained. "I'm sorry."

"No reason to be sorry. Better Lucas use it than someone else." She studied my face. "I remember you. You're the one who inherited Rick's place."

"Yes, ma'am."

"And you are the young woman who gave up her seat to me at the hospital on that terrible hot day."

"Yes. I was worried about you."

"Erma says you have questions about something David donated to the thrift store? Something Elmer picked up somewhere?" Jane's voice was thin but steady. "My Elmer was always bringing home things he thought useful."

Barbara hovered nearby, ready to intervene if her mother showed signs of fatigue. I noticed how her eyes never left the sleeping child, as if she expected Jane to drop him at any moment.

"We found something in a box I bought at the Harvest Thrift Store," Lucas said. "We're trying to find out where it came from."

"*Mamm,* maybe I should take Hudson to his crib," Barbara interrupted, reaching for the child.

"No." Jane's grip tightened protectively around the little boy. "He's fine. Let him stay." She turned to us. "Barbara watches over our little Hudson while her granddaughter works."

"The baby's name is Hudson?" Lucas asked, surprised.

"My great-granddaughter is *Englisch.*" Jane shook her head sadly. "She did not want to choose an Amish name for her son."

"Ah," Lucas said. "That explains it."

"This thing you found," Jane said to me. "Can you describe it?"

Lucas described the bridle—the quality of the leather, the silver work, the medallion that had surfaced from beneath decades of tarnish, and finally the insignia inscribed on it.

The more he talked, the more I watched the expression of welcome I'd seen on her face when we arrived, harden into something I could not read.

"Do you remember it?" I asked. "Do you know where he might have gotten it?"

Jane had gone very still. Even her gentle patting of the baby stopped. The morning light slanted through the sparkling-clean windows. I could almost feel the weight of whatever thoughts she seemed to be working through.

"Yes," she said. "I know where he got it."

She knew? That was wonderful! But something was wrong. She did not seem at all pleased with her knowledge.

Lucas allowed the silence to stretch between us, while Jane looked down at the baby and traced the curve of his ear with one finger.

"Is it time, little one?" she asked of the sleeping child.

"Time for what, *Mamm?*" Barbara asked.

Jane continued to wrestle with something in her mind.

"The problem with words," she said, "is that once they are spoken there is no bringing them back."

"That is true." Lucas said.

I did not speak. It was best that Lucas lead this conversation—but I was getting the impression that this conversation was about to take a much different direction than we'd ever expected.

Barbara had been growing more and more agitated. "Do you need your medicine, *Mamm*? Is this too much for you? Do you want to go lie down?"

Jane ignored her. Instead, she looked straight at Lucas. "You had problems with Elmer."

"I did," he said.

"He thought you were rebellious. I did not. I thought you were looking for answers."

"Thank you for that, Jane. You were right."

"Does anyone want coffee?" Barbara brought in a tray stacked with coffee cake and cups and a carafe of coffee, which she sat on the coffee table in front of us.

It was thoughtful of her to have baked, and typical of a visit to an Amish home—but I was not in the mood for a snack, and neither was Lucas. To refuse would be rude, however. Since Barbara was Jane's gatekeeper, both Lucas and I accepted a cup of coffee and a slice of cake we didn't want.

The coffee cake smelled of almonds and tasted like heaven. I made a mental note to refuse nothing edible offered in an Amish home.

"Your attitude was not all that Elmer and I disagreed about," Jane continued despite Barbara's tasty interruption.

"*Mamm*!" Barbara was obviously uncomfortable with the turn this conversation had taken. "Maybe Lucas and Amy should come back tomorrow… I think you are tired."

Jane, yet again, ignored her.

"My husband was a soldier!" Jane lifted her chin and blurted out those five words too loudly, as though she'd held them in so long, she'd spoken louder than she'd intended. She startled all of us, including the baby in her arms.

"*Mamm*!" Barbara said.

"Shhh," Jane said to the little one as she began to rock and pat. "It is okay. It is okay."

"*Daett* was a conscientious objector, like the other Amish men during the war." Barbara glanced at us apologetically, embarrassed by what she believed to be her mother's flight of fancy. "Please forgive my mother. Sometimes her mind wanders."

"I understand your husband was a faithful Christian soldier, Jane." Lucas tried to interpret her words. "Despite our differences, Elmer fought the good fight all the years that I knew him."

Jane's hands stilled now that the child was sleeping again. When she spoke again, her voice carried the authority of someone who had no patience for being dismissed.

"I may mix your name up with your brother David's sometimes, Barbara. But this I know to be true to the marrow of my very bones…" She fixed her daughter with a steady gaze. "Your father was a German soldier, and it is time someone knew what he went through because of it."

The words fell into the room like boulders tossed into a still pond. Barbara sank into a nearby chair, her face pale with shock.

"German? *Mamm*, that simply isn't true! Why are you saying these things?" She turned toward Lucas. "I wanted her to stay awake this morning for your visit, so I delayed her medicine this morning. I…"

"His name was Adelbert Jäger when I met him." Jane's voice was steady now, the decision made. "A boy caught up in Hitler's *Volkssturm*. The People's Storm, they called it. Young boys and old men were forced to fight at the end of the war because there were not enough able-bodied soldiers left to defend the country. They were untrained, badly provisioned, meant to be nothing but cannon fodder."

"*Mamm*! Please!"

Jane's voice hardened with old anger. "Elmer was only fifteen when they put him in uniform. There were others even younger than him—some no more than eight—given guns and sent to the front lines. Jane looked down at the sleeping child in her lap, then directly at me with eyes that held the weight of decades of silence, and I saw the awful truth in them. Barbara could not.

"My *Daett* was not a German soldier!" Barbara insisted. "That is ridiculous. He was Amish. He was a pacifist. He was American. Why are you saying these terrible things, *Mamm*?"

Jane rushed on—as though for fear Barbara would stop her from telling the whole story.

"He was fifteen years old when they put a uniform on him," Jane repeated. "Back before he became Elmer Yoder. Before he was Amish. When he was still Adelbert Jäger. I'll never forget his eyes the first time I met him. They looked like they had witnessed the end of the world—and in many ways they had."

The child on her lap seemed to sense the tension in the air again. He stirred, breaking Jane's concentration. He sat up and gazed into his great-grandmother's eyes for reassurance. Touched her face. Jane kissed his hand, and her voice softened. "It's alright, little one. *Gross-mammi* is here. Everything is fine."

"You're wrong, *Mamm*," Barbara continued to insist, shaking her head back and forth—a child who wouldn't listen to reason. "This is the ministroke talking. You've gotten mixed up in your head."

"He was in the Hitler Youth," Jane continued, as if her daughter hadn't spoken. "It was mandatory. To refuse to fight would mean execution."

Barbara was on the verge of tears. I felt sorry for her.

"This is too much," she said. "I'm calling David."

"Your brother cannot change what happened," Jane said simply. "Cannot change the regret your father carried all those years, either."

Barbara stood up abruptly. "This conversation needs to stop. Mamm is not well."

"We'll go now." Lucas stood to leave, and I followed. "Thank you for seeing us, Jane. And thank you for the excellent coffee cake, Barbara."

Jane looked at her daughter with love, but also with infinite sadness. "I know this is hard to hear, *dochter*. But some truths cannot stay buried forever. It has been a heavy burden to me, but I was obedient to Elmer's decisions. I always told Elmer I would hold his secret—but that I would not lie. Lucas and Amy asked a direct question. I gave them an honest answer."

Barbara walked us to our car, her face still pale with shock.

"I don't know what's going on with her," she said fretfully. "Why would *Mamm* make something like this up? Why would she say such terrible things about my father?"

"Maybe she's not making it up," Lucas said gently.

Barbara looked at him with eyes burning with anger. "If what she says is true, then everything I ever thought I knew about my father is a lie!"

"Not everything, Barbara," Lucas said with such compassion in his voice, it made me tear up. "It does not matter what he was forced to do as a boy, he became a good man. He tried hard to lead our church well."

She did not answer. She turned her back and strode back to the house. I felt sorry for Jane and the conversation I knew she was now facing with her daughter.

As we drove home, I wondered if Jane Yoder had truly opened a door to a hidden past, or if she was—as her daughter seemed to think—just an old woman in the beginning stages of dementia with a wild imagination.

"What do you think?" I asked Lucas. "Is her mind slipping?"

"Of course not."

"How can you say that for sure?"

"I've known her my whole life, and Jane's mind was as clear as spring water today," he said. "That woman was telling the truth."

CHAPTER 31

The kitchen felt different when Lucas and I returned from our conversation with Jane. What had been our cheerful conspiracy room an hour earlier now seemed inadequate for the weight of what we'd learned. Brady was replacing a washer in the sink faucet while Desiree sat at the table, braiding wildflowers into a crown with the focused attention of someone trying not to think.

Zelda looked up from her laptop as we entered. "How did it go?"

I sank into my chair, suddenly exhausted. "Jane Yoder said Bishop Elmer was a German soldier."

The words hung in the air. Brady's wrench clattered against the sink. Desiree stopped working on her flower crown. Zelda slowly and deliberately closed her laptop.

"What exactly did she say?" Zelda asked, her voice carefully neutral.

Lucas sought his chair with the deliberate movements of someone processing a great shock. "His real name was Adelbert Jäger. When he was fifteen, he became part of something called the *Volkssturm*."

"And before that, the Hitler Youth," I added.

Desiree set her flowers down. "Oh, dear."

"This is exactly the kind of thing Nolan Blackwood has been looking for," Brady said. "Former Nazi as Amish bishop. He couldn't ask for a better story."

"If any of it is true," I added. "Jane is ninety-five. She's had a stroke. Maybe she's confused, maybe her memory is—"

"Her memory is clear," Lucas interrupted.

Brady pulled an earpiece out of his ear. "I've been listening to Nolan Blackwood's podcast."

"And?" I asked.

"Its name is True History—but it's not. If you listen to one of the podcasts all the way through, you'll realize it's really built on his own obsession with conspiracies. The thing that worries me most is that a lot of his so-called journalism is basically 'gotcha' interviews where he blindsides people with accusations, then deliberately runs out of time before they can defend themselves. If he gets hold of this information, he'll milk it for all he can get—and who knows what repercussions it will have for the Amish community."

Zelda looked at us over her reading glasses. "The *Volkssturm* was very real. So was the Hitler Youth program that preceded it."

"Please tell us what you know," Lucas asked.

Zelda's expression grew somber. "The Hitler Youth started in the 1920s as what appeared to be a good thing. A positive and healthy youth organization. Camping, athletics, group singing, community service. Parents saw it as character building for their children and approved it enthusiastically."

"Wait, a moment." She pulled up something on her screen, then turned the laptop so we could see grainy black-and-white photographs of children in uniform, smiling and healthy-looking.

"It was fun at first. That was the point. Get the children involved, make them feel special, make them feel like they are part of something important."

"When did it change?" I asked.

"By the mid-1930s, membership became mandatory. The activities shifted from hiking and sports to military drills and ideological indoctrination." She scrolled through more images—the smiling children were replaced by stern-faced boys with wooden rifles. "Then they started sending them to fight."

Brady's face was grim. "How young?"

"There's documented evidence that boys as young as 8 years old were armed and put into combat situations during the final desperate months of the war."

Brady groaned.

"That's exactly what Jane told us," I said. "It sounded unbelievable."

"Toward the end, the *Volkssturm* routinely conscripted boys as young as twelve," Zelda said. "That was routine. Given a uniform, a rifle, maybe half a day of training, then they were sent to face Soviet tanks. It was a slaughter."

The kitchen fell silent except for the tick of the mantel clock. I thought about the man who'd disciplined Lucas for questioning church doctrine and tried to reconcile that image with a fifteen-year-old boy forced to fight.

"If this is true," Desiree said slowly, "if Bishop Elmer was Adelbert Jäger, then we're dealing with something much more complicated than an accidentally acquired artifact."

"We're dealing with a tragedy," Lucas said. "A child caught up in something he couldn't understand or control—trying to stay alive."

"That's not how Nolan Blackwood will tell it," Brady pointed out. "Trust me. I've been listening to him all morning. He'll make it sound like a Nazi war criminal infiltrated the Amish community and then spent decades fooling everyone while setting up some sort of white supremest organization."

"Jane said he regretted it until the day he died," I said. "What if we could prove that? What if we could prove Elmer Yoder spent his entire adult life trying to atone for things he was forced to do as a child?"

"How?" Desiree asked.

"By investigating his life here. His actions as a bishop, the way he served the community, the choices he made." I looked around the table. "If he really was trying to make amends, there would be evidence."

Zelda reached for her notebook. "We would need documentation. Immigration records, church records, testimonials from community members who knew him."

"But that would mean confirming that Jane's story is true," Brady said. "Are we prepared for that? What if we dig into this and find out Elmer Yoder was hiding something terrible he'd done back in Germany, even though he'd been forced to do it?"

The question hung heavy in the room. Through the window, I could see chickens pecking peacefully in the yard, Zedekiah strutting among them like an arrogant feathered dictator, and Rusty lying on the porch napping. Farm life continued while we grappled with the possibility that everything we thought we had known about this community's leader might be wrong.

"There's something else to consider," Lucas said. "If word gets out that we're investigating Bishop Elmer's past, it could tear this community apart. There are people who respected him, followed his leadership for decades. Finding out he was German, that he'd been in the Hitler Youth…"

"Even if he was just a child?" I asked.

"Some people won't make that distinction. They'll feel betrayed, lied to." Lucas's expression was troubled. "And others will say it explains his harshness, his rigid interpretation of the *Ordnung*… and they would probably be right."

Desiree had been listening with the attention of someone weighing options. "We have two choices. We can try to bury this, hope Jane doesn't tell anyone else, and pray Nolan Blackwood never finds out where that bridle really came from. Or we can control the narrative."

"What do you mean?" I asked.

184

"We investigate thoroughly, find the complete truth, and tell the story ourselves—with context, with compassion, with all the complexity that Blackwood would ignore." She looked around the table. "We turn this from 'Nazi Bishop Fools Amish Community' into 'Child Soldier Finds Redemption Through Faith and Service.'"

"That's good, assuming the second one is true," Brady said.

"Then we'd better find out as much as possible and quickly," Zelda said firmly. "Because in a few days, Nolan Blackwood will be podcasting to his five hundred thousand dedicated conspiracy junkies. The question is whether it will be based on the facts we've verified or sensational speculation he's invented."

My phone rang. It was Erma. I put her on speaker. "Jane wants to see you again tomorrow. She says there is more to tell. She wants you to have all the information, not just the little she was able to say before Barbara asked you to leave."

"She's not finished," I said to the others in my kitchen.

"Then we go back," Lucas said. "We listen to everything she has to say, and we figure out how to handle the truth—whatever it turns out to be."

"Make sure you record it, Amy," Desiree said. "Like you do for interviews for your books. You need to capture every word."

As we dispersed, each of us carrying our piece of an increasingly complex puzzle, I wondered if Jane Yoder had any idea what she'd set in motion with her decision to speak the truth.

Tomorrow we'd find out just how deep Bishop Elmer's secrets ran, and whether seventy years had been long enough to transform a boy soldier into the man, this community had trusted to lead them.

CHAPTER 32

J ane Yoder was waiting for us in the living room when we arrived
the next morning, but she wasn't alone. David Yoder, the son
who'd been cleaning out Bishop Elmer's farm, sat beside her.

"Barbara contacted me last night," David said by way of greeting.
His voice carried the careful neutrality of someone trying to process
impossible information. "She said my mother was telling stories about
my father being German."

"They're not stories," Jane said, her fingers worrying the edge of
her apron. "And it's time you heard the truth about the man who
raised you."

David's face showed a mixture of skepticism and concern. "Mom,
you've been under a lot of stress since the move. Maybe your
memory—"

"My memory is fine." Jane's voice sounded fretful. "What I told
these young people yesterday is true. What I'm going to tell you now
is also true." She looked at him, unflinching, but obviously hurt that
neither he nor Barbara believed her. "This story has been strong
within me for seventy years. I know this story like I know my own
face."

I noticed there was no coffee set out this morning, nor was there the scent of coffee cake baking. Apparently, Barbara no longer considered this a social visit.

"There were good reasons for Elmer wanting to keep this a secret. But if I'm going to tell his story now, I want to tell the whole story." Her gaze included David and Barbara. "What *really* happened."

Her daughter sat rigid, refusing to meet her eyes or ours.

"Barbara, please get me some water. I will need it."

Jane adjusted herself back in her rocking chair and gripped the armrests with both hands. When she spoke again, her voice took on the cadence of someone who'd rehearsed this story in her mind for decades—afraid she'd forget the details that mattered.

"The war was ending in the spring of 1945." Her voice grew distant, as if she were seeing through Elmer's fifteen-year-old eyes. "Adelbert's unit was stationed at a place called Hostau. Not a battle line—a horse farm. They'd moved hundreds of the most precious horses in the world there to keep them safe from the bombs falling on Vienna."

"What horses?" David asked, despite himself.

"The kind that men had spent three hundred years creating," Jane said simply. "Lipizzaner stallions from the Spanish Riding School. Horses trained to dance like angels, bred to be perfect. There were Arabian mares too—bloodlines that went back to the time of kings."

She paused, gathering strength. "But the Americans were coming from the west, the Russians from the east. Everyone knew the war was lost. The question was who would reach the horses first."

"Why did that matter?" Barbara asked reluctantly.

Jane's eyes hardened. "Because the Russian soldiers were starving. They'd already slaughtered the horses at another farm earlier in the war—cut them up for meat while the trainers wept and begged."

The room went silent while everyone absorbed that piece of information. Jane wasn't pulling any punches.

"The director of the riding school—Colonel Podhajsky—he

contacted the Americans. Asked for help to evacuate the horses." Jane's voice grew stronger. "But he needed help from the Germans who were stationed there. Some of them were young boys like Adelbert."

Jane took a sip of water.

"My husband told me once that he had two choices that day. He could follow orders and stay at his post, let whatever happened happen. Or he could risk being shot as a traitor and help save something beautiful."

"He chose the horses," Lucas said, with reverence.

"He chose to do what was right over loyalty to a regime he'd never believed in," Jane corrected. "Adelbert and several others volunteered, even knowing they could be executed if they were caught helping the Americans."

"How many horses?" David asked.

"Over a thousand. Can you imagine?" Jane's eyes grew bright. "They had to move them thirty-five miles through territory where anyone could have hurt them—German deserters, Soviet forces, partisan fighters. Some mares were heavy with foal and had to be loaded into trucks because the journey was too rough."

She paused, lost in the memory of Elmer's telling.

"Adelbert said it was like moving a river of living silk through hell. Three days of sleeping in the open, watering horses at streams, praying they wouldn't run into SS patrols who would shoot them all as deserters."

"But they made it," Amy said.

"They made it." Jane smiled through her tears. "Delivered every single horse safely to General Patton's forces. The Americans were so grateful to the young German soldiers who'd risked their lives—they treated them with honor even though they were prisoners of war."

"If this is true, after the war," David murmured, his voice barely audible. "How did *Daett* end up here?"

Jane's expression softened. "Your father was sent to a displaced persons camp. That's where he learned his grandfather had died—the only family he had left. A Lutheran pastor helped him find sponsors in America. Many Mennonite families needed farmhands after losing so many young men to the war."

She looked at David with infinite tenderness. "He was eighteen when I met him at a refugee center in Lancaster County. Still a boy, really, but carrying guilt that belonged to grown men."

"Why guilt?" Barbara whispered.

"The Hitler Youth wasn't just singing and marching, daughter." Jane said. "They made children report on their parents, their neighbors. Turn in people who spoke against the party. Adelbert had done those things—not because he believed in them, but because refusing meant death."

David's face crumpled. "He was just a child."

"A child who'd been forced to choose between survival and conscience every day for years." Jane reached over and took her son's hand. "He spent the rest of his life trying to make up for things that were never his fault to begin with."

"Is that why he was so hard on me?" David's voice broke.

"Probably." Jane stroked his knuckles with her thumb. "After seeing his country fall into evil, minor infractions felt dangerous to him. He'd seen how quickly good people could be turned into monsters when they were forced to stop paying attention to right and wrong."

"The bridle?" Lucas asked. "Why did he keep it?"

"Evidence that it had really happened. The experience was so profound he was afraid someday he might think he'd imagined it all."

"Where did he keep it?"

"In his workshop, in an old drawer. Sometimes when the nightmares were bad, he'd go out there and look at it. Remember that he'd chosen beauty over fear that day. He'd loved the mare it had been made for but hated seeing her wear the Nazi insignia. He was given permission to keep it because of his help with the rescue."

"Tell us the rest, *Mamm*," David prodded. "What happened after the Mennonites sponsored him?"

"He became Elmer Yoder instead of Adelbert Jäger. Joined the Amish church—its strictness appealed to him after living through so much chaos. We met while I was working as a hired girl for the same people who had sponsored him. We moved here to Tuscarawas County because land was cheaper than in Pennsylvania in those days, and fewer people asked questions about where you'd come from."

Jane paused, looking at each face around her, wanting to make certain everyone understood what she was trying to say.

"He wasn't running from justice—he was running toward peace. Toward a life where his children would never have to choose between survival and conscience. Where they'd be taught that violence was never the answer, no matter what."

No one had much to say after that.

I clicked off my recording app—which Jane had given me permission to use. Barbara helped her mother to bed, the conversation having drained every ounce of Jane's strength. As we prepared to leave, David walked us to the car.

"I wish I'd known," he said, his voice hollow. "All those years I thought he was just a rigid man who couldn't be pleased."

"He was protecting you the only way he knew how," Lucas said. "In his own way, he was trying to protect all of us."

CHAPTER 33

The deadline loomed: Nolan Blackwood had teased his audience with promises of an exclusive story about his discovery of a Nazi war criminal who had hidden his crimes within Amish farm country, and my kitchen had transformed into a makeshift newsroom under deadline pressure.

Desiree sat at one end of the table with her phone, laptop, and a legal pad covered in notes, working her way through a contact list that read like a Hollywood directory. Zelda occupied the other end with her laptop, multiple notebooks, and what appeared to be half the Austrian Cultural Ministry's email database spread across the screen.

"Yes, Dr. Kessler, I understand the time difference," Zelda was saying into her phone, checking her watch. "But this is urgent. We need official authentication within forty-eight hours."

At the same time, Desiree was speaking into her own phone with the smooth authority of someone who'd spent decades navigating media politics. "Jack, darling, I need a favor. Remember when I helped you with that disaster in Cabo? Well, now I need you to help me place a story with someone who understands the difference between true journalism and cheap sensationalism."

I sat between them with my laptop open to a blank document, trying to focus on the story I needed to write while coordinating interviews and fact-checking. The cursor blinked accusingly at me from the empty page.

Lucas appeared in the kitchen doorway. "Jane Yoder says she can see you again this afternoon. But David will be there too—he has questions about his father's immigration records."

"Perfect. I need more details about the timeline, about how Adelbert became Elmer." I looked up from my laptop. "What about the community? Any word from Bishop Noah?"

"He's calling a meeting with the church elders tonight. Wants to prepare them for what might be coming." Lucas took a chair beside me. "Some of the families are already asking questions. Word is spreading."

Desiree ended her call and looked up with satisfaction. "I've got three potential placements. *The Washington Post* has a columnist who specializes in WWII stories. *The Atlantic* is interested in a feel-good piece about redemption and forgiveness. And *60 Minutes* is considering doing a segment about heroism in unexpected places."

"*60 Minutes*?" I stared at her. "That's huge."

"That's the point. If we can get Bishop Elmer's real story on *60 Minutes*, Nolan Blackwood's little podcast becomes irrelevant—even if it comes out first." Desiree's eyes gleamed with strategic satisfaction. "But we need the story written, fact-checked, and authenticated first."

Zelda hung up her phone and immediately began typing rapidly. "Dr. Kessler is expediting the authentication process. He's also connecting me with the Operation Cowboy historical archives in Vienna. Apparently, there are records of German personnel who assisted in the horse evacuation."

"Records with names?" I asked.

"Possibly. The Americans documented everything, including the identities of German soldiers who surrendered voluntarily." Zelda looked up from her screen. "If Adelbert Jäger's name is in those files, we'll have unshakeable proof."

Zelda's phone buzzed. She read the text message aloud.

"Ms. Bloom, this is Nolan Blackwood. I'll be in the Sugarcreek area in three days for live interviews. I still need that interview with you about the Nazi artifact."

"He's coming here," Brady said. He'd been managing logistics—fielding phone calls, coordinating schedules, making sure we all ate something resembling meals. "He's planning to grab his 'gotcha' interviews with unsuspecting locals, and he thinks he'll grab one with a Sotheby's expert."

"I wouldn't be saying what he wants," Zelda said with exasperation.

"It doesn't matter," Brady said. "He'll take two words from you and record them in a way that will make it sound like you support everything he's saying—or that you're hiding something."

"Let him come," Desiree said firmly. "By the time he arrives, we'll have the authentic story already placed with major outlets. He'll be playing catch-up to us instead of the other way around."

"But only if I can actually write something worth publishing," I said, staring at my still-blank document.

"Then stop overthinking and start writing," Desiree said with the authority of someone who'd dealt with deadline pressure for thirty years. "Think of it like this—just pretend you've been given the assignment of ghostwriting a very short biography of an old Amish farmer who had three extraordinary days rescuing a thousand horses. Easy peasy."

For a moment, Brady stared at her as if she were a stranger. Then he shook it off and continued to work.

Mom was right. I opened a new document and began:

In the spring of 1945, as Allied forces closed in on Nazi Germany, a fifteen-year-old boy named Adelbert Jäger faced an impossible choice...

The words flowed. Jane Yoder's story, combined with Zelda's historical research and my own understanding of the community that Bishop Elmer had served, created a narrative that I hoped was both deeply personal and historically significant.

While I wrote, Zelda coordinated with Vienna, gathering documentation and official endorsements. Desiree worked on her media contacts, building momentum for placement while carefully managing the story's timing. Lucas fielded calls from community members, explaining what was happening without revealing details that weren't ready for public consumption.

By mid-afternoon, I had a rough draft of the opening section. I read it aloud to the team:

"The young German soldier who would become Bishop Elmer Yoder spent three days in the spring of 1945 moving more than a thousand horses across thirty-five miles of contested territory, risking execution as a traitor to save innocent animals he believed deserved to live. Seventy years later, a Nazi bridle found in an Ohio thrift store would finally reveal the extraordinary story of how a boy forced into uniform became a man dedicated to peace."

"That's good. That's your lead," Desiree said immediately. "That paragraph will hook them."

"Dr. Kessler just sent preliminary authentication," Zelda announced, reading from her screen. "The bridle is definitely connected to the Hostau stud farm. He's found documentation of the evacuation, including references to 'young German personnel who provided help.'"

My phone rang. Jane Yoder's number.

"Amy," came Barbara's voice. "Now that she's started, Mother is remembering more things. Details about the journey to America, about how the Mennonites welcomed German POWs as farm laborers and many times treated them like family. She wants to tell you about his immigration to America while she still can."

"We'll be right there."

As Lucas and I prepared to leave for our third interview with Jane Yoder, I felt the familiar sensation of a story coming together—that moment when scattered facts form a coherent narrative. But this time, the immediate stakes were higher than any ghostwriting project I'd ever worked on.

We weren't just writing a story. We were fighting for the truth about a good man who'd spent his entire adult life trying to earn forgiveness for things he'd been forced to do by one of the most horrendous war machines ever known. We were protecting a community from sensationalized lies. And we were racing against someone who saw conspiracy and evil where we'd found heroism and redemption.

"Ready?" Lucas asked, holding the door open.

"Ready," I said, grabbing my recorder and notebook. "Where is your cane?"

"Oh." He glanced around until he spotted it leaning against the kitchen table. "I forgot."

He was feeling strong enough that he was forgetting his cane, which pleased me. But there wasn't time to focus on that. We had only six days left to change the narrative. Six days to tell the truth before someone else distorted it beyond recognition.

As we drove toward Jane Yoder's house, I thought about the power of stories—how they could build up or tear down, heal or harm, depending on who told them and why.

The question for me was whether truth could move fast enough to outrun sensationalism in a world that preferred simple villains to complicated heroes.

We were about to find out.

CHAPTER 34

S ix days later, the *Washington Post* story went live at six AM Eastern time with a headline that flooded my body with relief: "The Quiet Soldier: How a German Child Soldier Chose Heroism Over Hatred."

I sat at my kitchen table with my laptop open. My own words stared back at me from one of the nation's most respected news websites. Beside the article was a photograph Zelda had secured from the Austrian Cultural Ministry—a black-and-white image of young soldiers helping to move horses during Operation Cowboy, with a caption identifying one of them as "Private Adelbert Jäger, later known as Elmer Yoder of Sugarcreek, Ohio."

"It's beautiful," Lucas said, reading over my shoulder. He'd arrived with homemade bread and applesauce from his sister Martha.

"Think people will read it?"

"People are already reading it." Desiree appeared in the doorway, her phone in hand, wearing my flannel pajamas, with absolutely no makeup, and with her hair tousled and uncombed. "The story's been shared over two thousand times in the first hour. #QuietSoldier is trending on social media."

I refreshed the page and watched the comment count climb steadily. Most responses were positive—people moved by Bishop Elmer's story, praising his courage in saving the horses, expressing admiration for his lifelong dedication to peace.

"What about Blackwood?" I asked.

"Posted his podcast at midnight, six hours before your story went live." Desiree's smile was sharp with professional satisfaction. "It's getting destroyed in the comments. People are calling him out for spreading conspiracy theories about a documented war hero."

Brady came in from his RV, looking more rested than he had in days. "I just talked with David Yoder. Jane has agreed to do interviews with two local news anchors tomorrow."

"Jane agreed to interviews?" I was shocked. The old lady was gutsier than I'd suspected.

"David says his mom is so relieved that her big secret is out, he thinks it's given her a new lease on life. She told him she wants to move back into her house now that he's gotten it all nice and cleaned out. He says he thinks she's also a little tired of Barbara."

A smile of deep satisfaction spread across Zelda's face. "I believe my work here is done, children. There is a bed in the next room with my name on it. I intend to sleep until I don't want to sleep anymore."

She turned off her computer, shuffled her notes into a neat stack, and with a wave of her hand, disappeared into the second guestroom.

"That sounds like a good idea," Desiree said. "I'll see you all later."

"Church starts at 8," Lucas said. "It isn't far. I have just enough time to get ready and make it."

"I'll hitch your buggy up," Brady said. "Then I've got animals to feed."

As they left, Rusty rose and followed them. At the door, he turned to look at me as though saying, "Will you be okay if I go next door?"

"I'll be fine, Rusty," I said. "You go on with Lucas."

I prepared to savor the comments pouring in about the article I'd written. It felt strange to have something published under my own name—to no longer be invisible—but I liked it more than I expected.

CHAPTER 35

Monday morning, familiar voices and laughter preceded the knock at his door as Lucas finished breakfast. He made his way to the front entrance, moving steadily now without his cane.

"*Guder mariye*, little brother," Regina announced, pushing past him into the kitchen with the confidence of someone who'd been bossing him around his entire life. As the second-oldest and most forceful, she'd appointed herself spokesperson when Martha wasn't available. Behind her came Susan and Ellen, each carrying covered dishes and wearing expressions Lucas recognized—the look his sisters got when they'd decided something or someone needed fixing. He hoped it wasn't him.

"We brought you lunch," Susan announced, setting a still-warm casserole on his counter. "Martha says you've been living on soup and bread."

"Not entirely..."

"And we brought reinforcements," Ellen added, as three of Lucas's nephews came through the door, ranging in age from eight to twelve.

Lucas smiled as he watched Rusty make himself available for hugs and belly scratches.

"You know, for a dog that can scare away bad guys, he sure acts silly when these boys come around." Ellen dropped to the floor to add a few pats and belly scratches of her own.

"Uncle Lucas!" Benjamin, Regina's twelve-year-old, launched himself at him with enthusiasm. "How's that project of yours coming?"

"Just fine." Lucas ruffled the boy's hair, grateful that his nephew's hug didn't knock him off balance the way it might have a month ago. He also wished the boy had said nothing about the project. He tried to give him a warning look, but Benjamin didn't notice.

"Do you need me to go back to Weaver Leather Supply for you?" Benjamin asked eagerly. "Any more supplies you want? Can I see what you've done so far?"

"We'll talk about that later, Benjamin," he said. "Why don't you take Rusty and the other boys outside? Brady is probably doing something interesting. Go see."

The kitchen was filled with the organized chaos that usually followed his sisters. Susan took charge of reheating food while Ellen watched over the boys from the doorway. Regina took a good, hard look at him. She lived in Mt. Hope, forty-five minutes away, and didn't get to visit as often as the others.

"You've lost weight," Regina observed.

"I have, but I'm putting it back on," he assured her. "I've gained ten pounds since leaving the hospital."

"Another ten pounds would be good," she said.

"I'll try."

"Not having a beard makes you look different," Ellen added, studying his face with clinical interest. "Younger."

"*Englisch*," Susan said, and Lucas caught the note of concern beneath the word.

Lucas relaxed into his chair by the window, contentedly watching his sisters move about with the familiar efficiency of women who'd been taking care of things—and people—most of their lives.

"How's Gretchen doing?" he asked.

"Back on her feet and filled with energy now that the baby is here," Susan said. "The girls are thrilled with their new baby brother. Martha is with her today. We're all going over after we finish here."

"Gretchen was doing too much before the baby arrived, if you ask me," Regina said with a worried frown. "Trying to pack for their move to Erie, Pennsylvania."

"You disapprove?" Lucas asked.

"I think it's *dumm*—Samuel moving his wife and children to a town where they don't know anyone just so he can get training as a physical therapist assistant."

"He wants to work at that Shriners' hospital with children who need him, Regina," he said. "It's a noble thing to do."

"I know," she said grudgingly. "But she doesn't want to go so far away. He's got that good job at the sawmill. He also has Gretchen and four healthy *kinner*. Why can't he be content?"

"I don't know," Lucas said. "For some people, contentment is harder to achieve than for others."

"Speaking of contentment—sit down, everyone," Regina commanded, and all three women arranged themselves in his small living room. "We need to talk."

Lucas had been pretty certain this conversation was coming and had dreaded it. It was the one where his family tried to understand the changes in him and decide whether they could accept the man he was becoming.

"Martha told us about the bridle," Susan said without preamble. "About the podcast—whatever that is—and the newspeople and the questions."

"She also had some things to say about Amy," Regina added, her voice carefully neutral.

The room went silent. Lucas looked at each of his sisters—Regina with her practical authority, Susan with her gentle concern, Ellen with her laughter and desire for everyone to be happy.

"What about Amy?" he asked.

These women had helped raise him, had celebrated his baptism into the church, had supported him through his wife's death and his years of solitary grief. They had the right to ask him anything they pleased, but that didn't mean he appreciated being interrogated about Amy.

"Benjamin saw you two walking together yesterday," Regina said. "Said you were laughing and talking and walking close together."

Lucas didn't deny it. "We probably were."

"She's not Amish," Regina pointed out, not unkindly.

"No, she's not."

"You can only remarry someone who is Amish," she said.

"That is one of our many rules," he agreed.

"And you shaved your beard," Susan said. "That means something."

"*Ja*, it does."

Lucas could hear the boys horsing around on the porch, probably trying to decide what mischief to get into. Outside, he glimpsed Amy working in her garden, unaware that three of his sisters were apparently preparing themselves to decide his future right now, while sitting in his living room.

"Shaving my beard means I was in an accident, the beard won't grow back in several places, and I don't want to look strange walking around with half a beard. That's what it means."

"Are you leaving the church?" Regina asked. "That's what I really want to know. If you are contemplating such a terrible thing, you shouldn't let your family find out from other people."

"I don't know yet, Regina." The honesty of his answer surprised even him. "But the possibility has been on my mind for years."

"I knew it!" Regina said. "It's because of that *Englisch* woman, isn't it?"

"This has nothing to do with Amy. If Elmer Yoder were still here and still bishop, I'd probably already have left the church, or at least moved to a different district by now."

Regina's eyes grew wide. "You don't mean that."

"I mean it, sister. I love the Lord, but…" He picked up his Bible from the small table beside his chair—the Bible Amy had used, the one with the worn out cover. "I've read this book through every year since I was sixteen. I have questions about things we believe and do that Elmer refused to answer and shunned me for even asking. You are my sisters, and I will tell you the truth—I will always tell you the truth—I am *still* asking questions. I just don't ask them out loud anymore, because it doesn't do any good. I cannot help but have questions."

All three sisters sat in stunned silence.

"Why have you not said something about this before now?" Susan asked in a soft voice.

"Because it took being forced to sit and think for hours at a time while my body healed, to face what I actually thought and believed."

"So…" Ellen said. "What *do* you actually think and believe?"

"I'm still figuring that out, little sister."

"Well," Regina said, defeated. "If you lose your mind and leave the Amish church, there are some very nice Mennonite churches in the area. I suppose I could accept that."

It was such a Regina-type thing to say, he almost laughed. Instead, he said, "I love you, Regina."

"Oh, well." She sounded surprised and a little annoyed. "I love you, too, I guess. I just wish you didn't have to *think* so much."

"Bishop Noah isn't as strict as Bishop Yoder," Susan said hopefully. "I've heard there are some Amish churches that no longer shun those who leave if they attend another conservative church."

"There is that," Lucas agreed.

"Gretchen is expecting us," Regina said. "It's time we went."

"Thank you for coming." Lucas was grateful they were leaving. Talking to his sisters about his questions had left him more tired than he used to be after a day of plowing fields.

He watched his sisters and nephews walk away, taking their noise and concern and conditional acceptance with them. Not approval, but not rejection either, for which he was grateful.

Through the window, he could see Amy sweeping fall leaves off her porch as she told his family goodbye. Her movements were easy and purposeful. She didn't know what had just happened, and that was just as well. He was grateful to know that whatever choices lay ahead, he wouldn't be making them completely alone. His sisters might not understand everything about the path he was considering, but he believed they would walk beside him while he figured it out. He hoped Amy would, as well.

CHAPTER 36

B rady found Desiree in the garden at sunset, picking the last of the late produce before the predicted frost. She wore one of Amy's old work shirts and jeans that had seen better days, her hair caught back in a simple ponytail. She looked more like the girl he'd fallen in love with thirty years ago than the glamorous actress who'd arrived in a red convertible.

"Planning on doing some canning?" he asked.

"Amy and Erma are. I think they're trying out a new recipe for relish." She straightened, brushing dirt from her hands.

"I enjoy seeing you like this," he said. "In work shirts and jeans with garden dirt on your hands. You seem more at peace with yourself."

"It's been good for me to be here." She glanced around at the rolling hills as though memorizing them. "But I need to get back. In my business, it isn't wise to disappear for too long."

"We'll miss you. I'm grateful that you and I talked. It was overdue —I needed that."

Desiree moved closer, her expression uncertain in a way that reminded him of their early days together. "Brady, I need to ask you something, and I need you to be honest."

"Shoot."

"I'm leaving for Los Angeles tomorrow."

"Okay."

"Do you want to come with me?"

The question caught him off guard. "You're asking me to move to California?"

"I'm asking if you'd be willing to try again. Really try this time, with all our cards on the table and no more secrets between us."

Brady looked out over the farm that had become home, thinking about the life he'd begun building here, the relationships he'd formed, the sense of belonging he'd found in this unlikely place.

"What about your career? The premieres and parties and all that Hollywood business?"

"What about it? Brady, I've had my career, and it's been wonderful, but it's not everything anymore. I'll take fewer jobs. We can spend time together. You won't have to work as hard." She stepped closer, her voice growing husky. "You know what I realized during that fight we had?

"I seldom have any idea what's going on inside your head, Darla."

"The two best years of my life were the ones I spent with you, before fear and selfishness made me stupid."

"And now?"

"Now I'm thinking maybe we're both old enough and smart enough to do this right. To build something on who we really are instead of who people think we should be."

"Darla." Brady pulled her into his arms, marveling at how right she felt there after all these years. She did not resist.

"California, huh?" he said. "Think they need any rodeo consultants for the movies?"

"I think they need whatever you want to be," she said, and then she kissed him like they had all the time in the world to figure it out.

As a twenty-something, those kisses had made his mind go numb and his knees weak. He would have done anything for her—including climbing on bulls and clinging to their bone-jarring backs until he won enough money to buy her the world.

But he wasn't young anymore. In the intervening years, he'd learned a lot about what made people tick and about what was important to him.

"I love you, Darla," he said truthfully.

Her eyes lit up. "I love you, too, Brady. I'm so sorry for what I did. I promise I'll spend the rest of my life making it up to you."

"In California?"

"Of course!" She sounded excited. "I have a beautiful house out there. It overlooks the ocean. You'll love it. You won't have to work anymore. I'll buy you a horse—anything you want."

In the short time he'd known her as Desiree, he'd watched all the movies and TV episodes she'd been in that he could find, and he'd studied them. She was one of the best actresses he'd ever seen, and after a while, he'd figured out why—what made her better than so many others.

Somehow, no matter what part she played, she believed with all her heart that she was that person. It was eerie how utterly she became the character she portrayed. The woman could go from being an Appalachian coal miner's wife to British royalty. He wasn't surprised at the awards she'd earned. He was surprised she hadn't won more.

He also knew she had no idea she was playing a part now. With all her heart, mind, and soul, she truly thought she had found the love of her life again. She believed they'd live happily ever after in her mansion overlooking the ocean.

And it sounded like—if he was a very good boy—she'd even buy him a pony!

No thanks.

"I love you, Darla, and I always will. The frightened girl I found sleeping in a pile of straw in our barn will always be the love of my life."

Her eyes filled with love for him. She was practically glowing.

"But I'm not moving to Los Angeles."

"Then I'll get us a place here..."

"Go home, sweetheart. You've had a nice time. You've accomplished a lot. I love the way you've deepened your relationship with our daughter and helped this community, but I plan to stay here long enough to help Lucas and Amy get on their feet—and then I'm headed back to do what I do best—keeping young cowboys from spending their lives in wheelchairs."

"You don't mean that!" she said.

"My love—when I say something—I really mean it. You'd eat me alive if I moved to California, and you wouldn't even realize you were doing it. I won't risk giving you that much power over me."

It took a few moments for her to catch on that this was real. He watched her eyes go from misty and happy to thunderous fury.

He paid no attention to the words she flung at him as he walked away. She'd be back. He knew she would be back. There was no way Desiree Stanton would allow some cowboy like him to reject her.

In the meantime, there were chores to do, and he was looking forward to doing them.

CHAPTER 37

My phone rang while I was reviewing my notes from the latest interview with Jane Yoder, trying to piece together more details about Adelbert's journey to America. The caller ID showed Carolyn Walsh, and I answered quickly, hoping she had a ghostwriting job for me. My funds were getting quite low.

"Amy!" Carolyn said. "I just finished reading your *Washington Post* article about the Amish bishop. When did you learn to write like that?"

I blinked, surprised. "I've always written like that."

"Sure, but this was different. This has heart, soul, real emotional depth. It reads like..." She paused, and I could almost hear her mind working. "It reads like a true bestseller."

I was disappointed. I had been hoping for a job, not just a compliment—although compliments from my editor were very nice.

"Do you have another celebrity memoir? I'm ready to start."

"I'm calling to offer you something much better. Your own name on the cover. Your own book. Your own story to tell—from the point of view of a respectful outsider." Her voice was brimming over with excitement. "I've been thinking about this ever since I read your article. What you've uncovered about this Adelbert Jäger—this isn't just a newspaper story. This is a novel begging to be written."

I sat down hard in my kitchen chair. "A novel?"

"A historical novel, yes, but grounded in fact. The journey from Hitler Youth to Amish bishop—do you have any idea how unprecedented that story is? How could it illuminate everything we think we know about guilt, redemption, and the cost of survival?"

My mind was racing. "Carolyn, I'm not a novelist. I'm a ghostwriter."

"You are a storyteller who's been hiding behind other people's voices for too long." Her tone grew more serious. "I've been watching your growth. You have a gift for finding the human truth in complex situations, for making readers care about people they've never met. This Adelbert Jäger story—this is your chance to use that gift under your own name."

"But the research involved, the historical accuracy required—"

"Would be extensive, yes. But you've already done much of the groundwork. You have access to primary sources through Jane Yoder, historical documentation through your expert contacts, and a deep understanding of both the Amish community and the broader historical context."

I thought about all the stories I'd helped other people tell, all the times I'd sat in interviews wishing I could explore the deeper questions, follow the threads that led to more complex truths.

"What exactly are you envisioning?" I asked.

"A book that follows Adelbert's journey chronologically, but tells it with detailed scenes, character development, emotional depth. Start with the boy who loved horses on his grandfather's farm. Show how the Hitler Youth program gradually transformed him into something he never chose to become. The horror of the Volkssturm conscription, the impossible choices he faced. Even the boys younger than him he tried to protect."

Carolyn's voice was gaining momentum, and I could picture her pacing her office as she spoke, the way she did when a project truly excited her.

"Then the redemptive moment—his choice to save the Lipizzaner horses despite the risk to his own life. The displaced persons camps, the journey to America, the prejudice he faced as a German immigrant. The way Mennonite families sponsored refugees despite their own communities' suspicions about German loyalties."

"And his transformation into Bishop Elmer?"

"Exactly. Show how a boy who'd been forced to participate in evil devoted the rest of his life to trying to earn his own forgiveness. Explore the way trauma shaped his leadership style, his rigidity, his inability sometimes to show mercy to others because he couldn't forgive himself."

My mind was already beginning to envision scenes, to hear Adelbert's voice as a young man wrestling with impossible choices.

"Carolyn, this would be a massive undertaking..."

"Which is why I'm prepared to offer you a substantial advance. Enough to give you the time and resources you'd need to do this properly. This story deserves to be told with the depth and care you could bring to it. But more than that, you deserve the chance to tell a story that matters to you personally."

"I'd want to tell it honestly," I said. "Not romanticizing what he went through."

"That's what would make it powerful. Amy, there are hundreds of books about World War II heroes. There are very few about the children who were victimized by both sides, who survived trauma and transformed it into service."

"And you think there's a market for that?"

"I think there's a hunger for stories about ordinary people who choose to do extraordinary things in impossible situations."

"I'll call you back later," I said.

I hung up and didn't walk; I ran to Lucas's house—nearly bursting through the door before he could completely open it.

"Lucas! Guess what!"

He grinned. "What's Zedekiah done now?"

"No! Carolyn is offering me a job writing a novel based on Bishop Elmer's life!"

"That's wonderful!" His face lit up. "I'm so happy for you!"

Then I ran straight to Brady, telling him the same thing.

"Hurry up and get it written," he said. "I want to buy copies for all my rodeo buddies. They'll love it!"

I went to the house to boot up my laptop and get started. The thought struck me that when this was finished, there would be a launch, and book signings, and maybe even interviews. I searched inside myself to see if that bothered me. Nope. Not anymore. Somehow, my need for an invisibility cloak had disappeared.

CHAPTER 38

Lucas ran his hands over the completed leather bag as it sat on his kitchen table, admiring the tooled scene that had occupied his evenings for months. In the lamplight, the carefully-crafted image told its own story. The leather was light but would age to a rich honey color, and every detail was crisp and clear. Tonight, it was finished.

His fingers traced the tooled scene on the back pocket, showing the sunrise as he saw it every morning, overlooking the farm and Amy's porch. Hidden within the scene were small images that told Amy and Lucas' story. Zedekiah, the rooster with his crooked feathers, surveyed the land, looking much like he did after Lucas came to Amy's rescue when the bird attacked her the first day they met. A bucket of daffodils sitting by Amy's front door, like the bucket he had presented to her before she went back to New York. A cup of coffee on the banister of the front porch, where Amy inevitably left hers every morning as she greeted the day. The faintest hint of the outline of Brady's RV on the left side. An accumulation of the things that Amy and Lucas had shared.

As he looked at the finished image, he knew—with a certainty that cut through every doubt—that he loved her. Not the attraction he'd been fighting, not even their deepening friendship, but the kind of love that transforms everything it touches.

She had fought for his people. For traditions that weren't hers but had become precious because they were his. She'd done it not out of obligation, but from choice.

How could loving someone like that be a mistake?

The main compartment was currently unzipped, revealing the practical interior he'd spent weeks perfecting—laptop compartment sized precisely for her computer, dedicated pockets for her charging cord, pen holders along the sides, business card slots, a compartment for her phone.

He had kept the front pocket professional. Only her initials were visible in the bottom right-hand corner. But it was the tooled image on the back pocket that told their love story. The image holding a compilation of memories too precious to lose.

He would always be Amish at heart. The values of simplicity, service to God, service to family and community—these would remain his foundation. But maybe faithfulness didn't mean choosing between tradition and love. Maybe the most faithful thing was trusting that God's grace was big enough to bless what served His purposes, even when it didn't fit expectations.

Rusty lifted his head from his spot by the chair, watching Lucas with curiosity. The dog had become attuned to his moods during their months of healing together, and something in Lucas's stillness must have caught his attention.

"What do you think, boy?" Lucas asked softly. "Tomorrow, do I tell her everything?"

Rusty's tail thumped once against the floor—approval, or perhaps just happiness at being spoken to.

Through the window, he watched Amy move around her kitchen. She deserved the truth. She deserved to know that every scene had been created with love.

Tonight, he would sleep peacefully. He had decided that tomorrow evening he would show her what his hands and heart had been creating in secret—twelve squares of devotion, one man's attempt to capture love for all time in a handmade gift.

But before he did all that, he needed to get some sleep. Tomorrow was Sunday, and he planned on going to church.

CHAPTER 39

Lucas sat in his buggy outside the Walnut Creek Mennonite Church, his hands gripping the reins tighter than necessary. It was an off-Sunday for his district—the week when no Amish services were held, providing time for visiting or rest. Most people would spend the morning at home, reading Scripture or visiting with neighbors.

Instead, he was here, preparing to attend a Mennonite service.

The building looked so different from the plain homes, barns, and workshops where his people gathered. It was modern and spacious. Even the parking lot felt foreign—cars instead of buggies, families wearing clothes that were modest but *Englisch*, children carrying Bibles with bright covers.

A family walked past his buggy—the father carrying a toddler, the mother holding the hand of a little girl who skipped beside her. They looked peaceful. The woman wore a floral dress that would have scandalized Bishop Elmer, but there was nothing immodest about her appearance. Just… different.

Lucas tied off his reins and stepped down from the buggy, his heart hammering. He'd dressed carefully—plain dark pants, white shirt, no suspenders. Without his hat and freshly shaven, he knew he'd blend in.

The church foyer was definitely not a barn, or a basement, or a workshop. It was lovely. It had warm lighting, comfortable seating areas, and people stationed to welcome newcomers. A middle-aged woman approached with a smile.

"Good morning! I don't think we've met. I'm Sarah Yoder."

"Lucas Hershberger," he said.

"Aren't you Martha's brother?"

"I am."

"Wonderful! Are you looking for a Sunday School class, or would you prefer to go straight to the sanctuary?"

"Sanctuary, please. And… could I sit in the back?"

"Of course." She handed him a bulletin and pointed toward the main doors. "Service starts in about ten minutes. Coffee and fellowship afterward if you'd like to stay."

Lucas found a seat on the last pew, grateful for the relative anonymity. The sanctuary was beautiful in its simplicity—wooden pews with padded seats, white walls, a wooden cross hung above the stage area.

People entered with soft conversation and warm greetings. Families, elderly couples, young adults, children who seemed genuinely happy to be there. The atmosphere was reverent but not rigid.

The service began with singing—first an a cappella hymn that sounded familiar, then another with guitar accompaniment that lifted the voices in harmony. The music was beautiful, stirring.

The congregation stood for the next song, and a movement in the middle section caught his eye.

A woman was standing during the hymn, singing. She wore a simple cream-colored dress, nothing fancy, but something about her posture, the way she held herself, seemed familiar…

Lucas's breath stopped.

Amy.

She was here. In a Mennonite church. On a Sunday morning. Alone.

Why hadn't she told him she would be here? A dozen emotions crashed through him at once.

She hadn't seen him yet, focused as she was on the service. Lucas watched her take part in the responsive reading, noticed how comfortable she seemed, how naturally she followed along. This was obviously not her first visit.

The pastor began his sermon—something about faith and courage, about stepping outside familiar boundaries when God called you to grow. Lucas tried to focus on the words, but his attention kept drifting to Amy, three rows ahead and slightly to his left.

CHAPTER 40

I slid into the wooden pew at Walnut Creek Mennonite Church, opening my hymnal to the page announced from the pulpit. For three weeks now I'd come, ever since Desiree had flown back to California and Zelda left to tie up loose ends in New York. Each Sunday felt more like a homecoming than the last.

The decision had begun with those hours reading Lucas's Bible aloud during his recovery. I'd found myself drawn to words that seemed to speak to the restless hunger I'd been feeling for a long time. Something that went beyond career success or even the love I felt for Lucas.

Brady had offered to come with me, but something always seemed to come up—farm emergencies, phone calls from rodeo sponsors. I didn't mind coming alone. I found peace in the Sunday morning drive, the anticipation of worship.

The congregation rose for the opening hymn, and I stood with them, my voice joining a familiar melody I'd learned to love. I was reaching for the verse when someone slid into the pew beside me, close enough that I caught the scent of familiar soap and my heart stopped.

It wasn't possible.

Without looking, I knew. Somehow, impossibly, Lucas was here. In a Mennonite church. On a Sunday morning. Standing beside me.

His hand reached down to help hold my hymnal, his fingers brushing mine. The touch sent electricity up my arm, but more than that—the gesture was so intimate, so naturally partnered, that I nearly swayed with the implications.

I risked a glance at his profile. He wore plain clothes—dark pants, white shirt—but without his hat and suspenders, he looked like he belonged here. Like maybe we could belong here together.

The thought was so overwhelming I choked up and had to stop singing.

What did this mean? Why was he here, sharing my hymnal, taking part in worship that his own community no doubt viewed as too liberal, too *Englisch*? I'd not told him I was attending here. I'd kept it secret—because it was none of his or anyone else's business. This was my walk with God, still new and precious. I didn't want it to be the topic of discussion around the house—not until I knew more and was stronger in my faith.

When we bowed our heads for prayer, I felt his fingers slowly intertwine with mine.

I should have pulled away. Should have worried about who might see, what people might think, whether this was appropriate in a house of worship. Instead, I held on, marveling at how perfectly our hands fit together, how right it felt to be praying beside him.

What would it be like if this could be my reality for the rest of my life?

The thought came unbidden, painting pictures I'd been afraid to imagine. Sunday mornings like this, sharing worship and music and quiet moments of faith. A life built on the foundation of something larger than ourselves, blessed by a community that could embrace both tradition and growth.

The prayer ended, but Lucas didn't release my hand immediately. For just a moment longer, we sat connected in the peaceful sanctuary, surrounded by the gentle murmur of a congregation settling back into their seats.

I have no idea what the minister talked about.

When the service concluded and people began filing out, I turned to face him fully.

"Lucas?"

"Amy."

His smile was tentative but genuine. "Meet me back at the house as soon as you can. I have a gift for you."

A gift? "Of course."

CHAPTER 41

Lucas stepped onto his porch, grateful that his leg had fully healed, and began walking toward Amy's house, carrying weeks of carefully crafted love in his arms. The cloth-wrapped bundle felt substantial—good leather has weight to it, his grandfather had always said. That weight meant quality, durability, something made to last.

At Amy's front door, he paused one last time. Through the window, he could see her settling into her favorite chair with a cup of tea, that chaotic tote bag beside her on the floor, laptop cord snaking out like it was trying to escape.

Beautiful. She was so beautiful to him.

Lucas knocked softly and waited for her to answer, his heart hammering against his ribs.

Amy opened the door and saw the rectangular cloth-wrapped bundle in his arms. "Oh. Did you bring me chocolates?" She teased him. "I could really use a box of chocolates tonight."

He could hear the curious warmth in her voice. She stepped aside to let him in, watching as he carried his hidden creation to her coffee table.

"This is something I've been working on since the accident. I hope it is useful."

Lucas began unwrapping the cloth, revealing light brown leather that seemed to glow in her living room's early afternoon light. As more of the pockets emerged, Amy's gasp was audible, her hand flying to her mouth.

"Lucas, this is... this is... beautiful, but what is it?"

"All those evenings when I couldn't sleep," he said, opening the bag so she could see the full scope of what he'd created. "Weeks of trying to make something worthy of the woman who brought light and hope back into my life."

The bag unzipped like butterfly wings, revealing compartments perfectly sized for her laptop, notebook, pens, phone, and all the other necessities that currently lived in tote bag chaos. But Amy had turned the bag over and was staring at the back pocket, her fingers tracing the dimensional images that rose from the leather with startling clarity.

"Every moment we've shared has mattered to me," Lucas continued, his voice growing stronger as he watched recognition and wonder dawn on her face. "I wanted to preserve all of it in something that would last, something you could carry with you always."

Amy reached out to touch the panel showing the daffodils, her fingers following the careful tooling with something approaching reverence. The leather was warm under her touch, supple as silk but strong enough to protect what mattered most.

"You made this? Seriously, you made all of this?"

"My grandfather taught me leatherwork when I was a boy. I was good at it then, but I'd forgotten until..." He gestured toward her abandoned tote bag. "Until I watched you fight with that bag every day, digging for things, getting frustrated when you couldn't find what you needed."

"Tell me about this picture you've created," she whispered, moving closer. "I want to know every detail."

Lucas guided her through the tooled scene, his grandfather's techniques bringing their story to life in leather that would improve with age and handling.

"Zedekiah represents the morning after you inherited the farm. After I saved you from his spurs, and took him back to the pen, I saw you standing in the doorway like you were afraid to take on the farm but you were determined to try." He pointed to the rooster with his cockeyed feathers and puffed-up chest.

"And this quilt," he moved his finger to a blanket he had put over the swing on the porch, "is one of the quilts you would wrap yourself up in when you didn't want to ask me to start a fire the first winter you stayed here. "

She recognized each hidden image, each careful detail he'd preserved. Then she noticed something that took her breath away—herself. The outline was barely noticeable through the window of Rick's Study, and if she hadn't recognized it as herself, she would have thought it was a shadow.

"Why this?" she said softly.

"That window was where I looked for you every day after you left. It's where my eyes were drawn, hoping to steal another glance at you typing on your laptop, and having to face the reality that you were gone. That was when I discovered that what I felt for you was stronger than any fear I'd ever known." Lucas stepped closer, no longer able to maintain a careful distance. "Amy, every toolmark in this leather was me trying to hold on to something I thought I could never have."

Amy couldn't speak. The bag was a love letter written in leather, each image a memory he'd treasured enough to preserve forever.

"Lucas," she whispered.

"Amy, I want you to understand that I love you."

With mock seriousness, she said, "Does this mean you don't intend to chase down an Amish woman to marry you after all?"

Lucas laughed. "That's what it means."

Before she could respond, he framed her face with his hands. "May I kiss you?"

Instead of answering with words, she closed the distance between them, her lips meeting his in a kiss that carried months of suppressed longing and the promise of everything they might build together.

When they broke apart, Lucas rested his forehead against hers.

"I love you, Amy Stanton," he whispered. "Past reason, past wisdom, past any ability to change my mind about it."

The confession hung between them like something tangible, months of yearning finally given voice. Lucas waited, his heart hammering, while Amy processed what he'd said and what the bag represented.

Everything depended on what happened next. Everything he'd been building toward, everything he'd been afraid of risking, came down to this moment and whatever choice she would make.

"I love you too," she replied, her hands fisting in his shirt to keep him close. "Enough to figure out how to make this work, whatever it takes."

They stood together in her living room, surrounded by the knowledge that everything had just changed forever.

From the doorway came a soft whine. Rusty sat watching them, his head tilted as if trying to understand the shift in the air around his two favorite people. When Amy looked at him, his tail began a tentative wag.

"I think he approves," Amy said softly.

"He has good judgment," Lucas replied, pulling her close again.

EPILOGUE

The evening light slanted through the kitchen window, casting long shadows across the worn linoleum floor that Jane Yoder had mopped every day for fifty-three years. At ninety-five, her movements were slower now, but her hands still knew their way around this house that had been her home for more than half a century.

She carefully lowered herself into Elmer's chair—its wooden arms worn smooth by decades of use, the one where he'd read his Bible every morning and every evening until the day the Lord called him home. The seat cushion still held the impression of his body, and sometimes, in the gathering dusk, she could almost convince herself he was still there.

The house felt too quiet without him. No longer the comfortable rustle of pages turning, the soft sound of his coffee cup settling on the wooden table, the gentle clearing of his throat before he read aloud the verses that had spoken to his heart. For seventy years, their lives had moved together like two parts of the same song. Now she was learning to sing alone.

From her chair, she could see the entire front room—the simple wooden furniture Elmer had built with his own hands during their first years of marriage, the braided rug his sister had made for their wedding gift, the plain white walls that had never needed decoration because their life together had been ornament enough.

In her lap, Jane held something she'd kept hidden even from the children and grandchildren—a small cloth bag containing a single braid of horsehair, snow-white and coarse between her fingers. Elmer had brought it with him from Austria, cut from the mane of one of the Lipizzaner mares he'd helped save. He'd given it to her on their wedding night, a possession from the world he'd left behind.

"Did I do the right thing?" she whispered into the room, her voice barely audible above the ticking of the old clock. "Telling your story to that young woman?"

She'd been wrestling with this question for several weeks now, ever since Amy and Lucas had left with their notebooks full of the secrets that had been safe in her heart for so long.

What if her grandchildren, her great-grandchildren, heard their grandfather's story and thought it gave them permission to abandon the pacifism and faith that was the cornerstone of their people?

"You were forced to fight," she continued, stroking the horsehair braid with trembling fingers. "But you chose peace." Her voice caught. "I'll pray they understand the difference even after I'm gone and can no longer tell them."

The room grew darker as evening crept over the farmland outside. Soon it would be winter—her first winter alone. Sometimes she wondered if the Lord had simply forgotten about her, left her here while He called home everyone she'd ever loved. Her parents, her siblings, her dear friends, two of her children—all gone. And Elmer, her heart's companion, sleeping now in the cemetery.

"*Es wird net lang sei,*" she told him, lapsing into the Pennsylvania Dutch that felt more natural when she was tired. "It won't be long now until I see you again. My heart feels like it is wearing out. Like an old clock that's been wound too many times."

She wasn't afraid. At ninety-five, death felt more like a doorway than an ending. But she worried about leaving things undone, words unspoken, truths that might be misunderstood after she was gone.

A soft knock at the front door interrupted her conversation with memories. Jane's heart fluttered—visitors were unusual, and at her age, unexpected callers usually brought difficult news. She put the horsehair braid carefully back in its cloth bag and made her way slowly to the door, her cane tapping against the familiar floorboards.

Amy Stanton stood on the porch, carrying a brown leather bag and wearing a smile.

"Mrs. Yoder, I hope I'm not disturbing you. I know it's late, but I have something I'd like to show you, if you have a few minutes."

"*Ja*, of course. Come in, child." Jane stepped aside, noting how the younger woman moved with careful consideration, as if she understood hurried movements could startle an old heart.

Amy placed her bag on the kitchen table and opened it to bring out her laptop. "I've been doing a lot of research since our conversations, and I discovered something I thought you might like to see."

Jane watched with curiosity as Amy opened the machine and pressed several buttons. The screen flickered to life, brighter than anything Jane had seen outside of the electric lights at the hospital.

"This might seem strange," Amy said. "But I found a video of the Lipizzaner horses performing at the Spanish Riding School in Vienna. These are the descendants of the horses your husband saved."

The screen filled with images that took Jane's breath away. White horses, magnificent and powerful, moving with a grace that seemed to defy the laws of earth and gravity. They danced—there was no other word for it—their movements precise and flowing, like living poetry written in muscle and bone and ancient training.

"*Ach, mein Gott*," Jane whispered, sinking into her chair, unable to look away from the screen. "They are so beautiful!"

The horses performed movements that seemed impossible— leaping into the air with all four feet off the ground, dancing sideways with steps so delicate they might have been walking on clouds, turning and spinning with their riders as if horse and human had become one.

"Hundreds of years of breeding, of training these magnificent creatures to be some of the greatest war horses ever seen. And now, they no longer fight in wars. They bring beauty and joy to thousands of people who come to watch them perform."

Jane's eyes filled with tears as she watched the horses move across the screen like living dreams. "After the war," she said, her voice thick with memory, "the people in Vienna, they sent these horses to America. To say thank you for saving them."

"Really?"

"*Ja*, Elmer read about it in the newspaper. The horses were coming to perform in different cities—Chicago, New York, other places." Jane's voice grew stronger as she remembered. "He asked me if I thought it would be wrong for him to go see them. Such a long journey, and the expense..."

Amy listened intently.

"I told him he must go. That God had used him to save these beautiful creatures, and perhaps God wanted him to see what had become of them." Jane smiled through her tears. "He took the bus to Chicago. Gone for three days. I stayed at home with the children. When he returned, he could talk of nothing else."

On the screen, the horses continued their ethereal dance, their white coats gleaming under the lights of the grand arena.

"He said it was like watching angels," Jane continued. "The way they moved, the way they seemed to understand music, to feel the rhythm in their bodies. He said he finally understood why God had put him in that place, at that time. Not to serve in the army, but to serve the miracle of His creation. Elmer said that man creates the ugliness of war, but God creates only beauty."

Amy reached across the table and took Jane's fragile hand in her young, strong one as Jane continued to watch the screen through tears that made the dancing horses shimmer like visions.

"He was a good man. People think that because he was strict as a bishop, because he held firm to our ways, that he was harsh. But he understood what the world looked like when people wandered away from the church and forgot to choose peace over violence."

"I understand."

Jane squeezed Amy's hand with surprising strength. "When I am gone—and it will not be long now—I want you to tell them. Tell my grandchildren and my great-grandchildren. Tell them their grandfather knew the difference between being forced to serve evil and choosing to serve good. Tell them that following the teachings of Christ is not about being weak. It is about being strong enough to save what is just and kind and beautiful, even when the whole world has gone mad."

They sat together in the kitchen, watching the horses dance on the bright screen, two women separated by decades but united in their understanding of love, sacrifice, and courage.

As the video ended and the screen grew dark, Jane felt something she hadn't experienced since Elmer's death—total peace. The story was told now. The truth was safe in good hands. Whatever happened next, her beloved husband's legacy would be one of beauty preserved, not violence remembered.

"Danki," she whispered to Amy, but her eyes were looking beyond the young woman, beyond the kitchen walls, to a place where an old man with gentle hands was waiting to show her horses that danced like angels in meadows that never ended.

AUTHOR'S NOTE

When I began researching this story, I thought I was simply writing about a mysterious Nazi artifact found in Amish country. What I discovered instead was one of the most remarkable chapters of World War II—Operation Cowboy, the daring rescue of over a thousand horses from Czechoslovakia in 1945.

This extraordinary mission was real. American forces, working with German officers who risked execution for treason, successfully evacuated the world's most precious horses from the path of advancing Soviet forces. Some of the German personnel were nothing more than teenagers conscripted into the Hitler Youth and later the Volkssturm—boys, under the threat of execution, made to wear uniforms they never chose, fighting in a war they didn't understand. Many carried guilt for decades over things they were forced to do to survive.

The Amish and Mennonite communities did indeed sponsor many German refugees and displaced persons after the war, despite facing suspicion about their own loyalties due to their German heritage and pacifist beliefs. Their willingness to extend grace to former enemies exemplifies the radical forgiveness at the heart of their faith.

The Spanish Riding School in Vienna continues to this day, and the Lipizzaner horses still perform their breathtaking displays of classical dressage. They are living monuments to the power of beauty preserved, even in humanity's darkest hours.

While Amy and Lucas's love story is fiction, it represents a truth I've witnessed repeatedly in my research and writing: that obeying

God's will sometimes requires us to step beyond the boundaries we thought defined us, and that the most profound faithfulness sometimes looks nothing like what others expect.

And to the real child soldiers of every war, both military and domestic, may you find the peace that comes from understanding *survival is not sin* and that God's grace can transform the deepest shame into a life that becomes something beautiful.

To anyone wishing to learn more about Operation Cowboy—I highly recommend Elizabeth Lett's extraordinary book, *The Perfect Horse*.

-Serena

PENNSYLVANIA DUTCH GLOSSARY

Holmes County Deitsch is largely an oral tradition with few official written standards. As such, spellings used in the glossary aim to reflect pronunciation and usage, not standardized orthography. Variation among speakers is natural and expected.

Ach - Oh; an exclamation
Alle - All
Avek gerannt - Ran away
Awwright - All right
Bischt du - Are you
Blumen - Flowers
Boppli - Baby
Bruder - Brother
Bu - Boy
Daadi Haus - Grandfather house; smaller dwelling on Amish property for older family members
Daett - Father/Dad
Danki/Denki - Thank you
Die kinner - The children
Dochter - Daughter
Du bischt - You are
Erde - Earth, soil
Es wird net lang sei - It won't be long
Geh mit der - Go with the
Geld - Money

Gewiss net - Certainly not

Glaeder - Clothes

Grossmammi - Great-grandmother

Gut - Good

Gviss - Certain, definitely

Hab dich gekannt - Knew you

Haus - House

Ich - I

Ja - Yes

Kapp - Prayer cap/bonnet

Kinner - Children

Komm schnell - Come quickly

Kumm - Come

Mamm - Mother/Mom

Meedlies - Girls

Mei - My

Mein Gott - My God

Mei sohn - My son

Mir bete - We will pray

Nee - No

Net - Not

Nimm net zu viel - Don't take too much

Recht - Right, correct

Schweschder - Sister

Siebetsen - Seventeen

Un - And

Varst - Were

Ven du varst yung - When you were young

Wort - Word

Yah - Yes (alternative spelling)

Yung - Young

ALSO BY SERENA B. MILLER

SECRETS OF SUGARCREEK SERIES

- A Stranger for Christmas (Book 1)
- Searching for Samuel (Book 2)
- The Quiet Soldier (Book 3)

LOVE'S JOURNEY IN SUGARCREEK SERIES

- The Sugar Haus Inn (Book 1)
- Rachel's Rescue (Book 2)
- Love Rekindled (Book 3)
- Bertha's Resolve (Book 4)
- The Heart of Sugarcreek (Book 5)

LOVE'S JOURNEY ON MANITOULIN ISLAND SERIES

- Moriah's Lighthouse (Book 1)
- Moriah's Fortress (Book 2)
- Moriah's Stronghold (Book 3)
- Eliza's Lighthouse (Book 4)
- Moriah's Lighthouse Collection (Books 1-3)

MICHIGAN NORTHWOODS HISTORICAL ROMANCE

- The Measure of Katie Calloway (Book 1)
- Under a Blackberry Moon (Book 2)
- A Promise to Love (Book 3)

ALSO BY SERENA B. MILLER

ABOUT THE AUTHOR

SERENA B. MILLER is a power-house in both publishing and television, earning her place as a *USA Today Bestselling Author* and collecting prestigious honors including the Romance Writers of America **RITA**, the American Christian Fiction Writers **CAROL**, and recognition as a **CHRISTY** Award finalist. Her signature storytelling first leaped from page to screen when *The Sugar Haus Inn* from her *Love's Journey in Sugarcreek* series became the award-winning UPTV movie *Love Finds You in Sugarcreek*, capturing the coveted **Templeton Epiphany Award**. Her mastery of heartfelt narratives has since inspired two acclaimed Hallmark Channel features: the compelling *An Uncommon Grace* and the captivating *Moriah's Lighthouse*, the latter drawn from her *Love's Journey on Manitoulin Island* series and set against the stunning backdrop of coastal France.

For More Information, Please visit serenabmiller.com

facebook.com/AuthorSerenaMiller

x.com/Serenabmiller

instagram.com/serenabmiller

amazon.com/author/serenabmiller

bookbub.com/authors/serena-b-miller

goodreads.com/SerenaBMiller

Printed in Dunstable, United Kingdom